At the end of practice, Coach Matthews says he'll call us tomorrow to tell us if we're on the A or B Team. Then we have to line back up for touch-and-goes again, and my legs already burn from being sore on sore, and I don't want to breathe one more breath into this helmet. And it makes me wonder again about Parker, if he's in a cage and feels shut in and too hot and just wants to get out. I wish Dad would give in and take me to the humane society so I could see for myself and let Parker rest on my shoulder for just one second more.

Also by Lindsey Stoddard

Just Like Jackie

Right as Rain

Bea Is for Blended

BRAVE LIKE THAT

LINDSEY STODDARD

HARPER

An Imprint of HarperCollinsPublishers

Library of Congress Cataloging-in-Publication Data

Names: Stoddard, Lindsey, author.

Title: Brave like that / Lindsey Stoddard.

Description: First edition. | New York, NY : HarperCollins, [2020] |

Summary: Eleven-year-old Cyrus knows he is not cut out to be a football
    hero or fireman like his adopted father, but it takes a skittish stray dog
    to teach him that he, too, can be brave.

Identifiers: LCCN 2019040574 | ISBN 978-0-06-287812-0

Subjects: CYAC: Self-actualization (Psychology)—Fiction. | Fire
    departments—Fiction. | Dogs—Fiction. | Reading disability—Fiction. |
    Middle schools—Fiction. | Schools—Fiction. | Orphans—Fiction.

Classification: LCC PZ7.1.S7525 Br 2020 | DDC [Fic]—dc23

LC record available at https://lccn.loc.gov/2019040574

Typography by Sarah Nichole Kaufman

21 22 23 24 25   PC/BRR   10 9 8 7 6 5 4 3 2

First paperback edition, 2021

*For Miles and Paige
May you always listen to what's deep
down in you.*

CHAPTER 1

Doorstep

Parker comes to us on my birthday. The end of summer. The night before football tryouts.

When we hear him whimper and whine at the firehouse front door, all the guys stop what they're doing. Roger puts down the kitchen knife. Leo drops a last potato in the big pot. Mike quits his story mid-sentence. Dad sits up straight. And I know what they're all thinking because I know the guys. They're thinking about August twenty-seventh eleven years ago. When I showed up at the firehouse doorstep as a screaming, crying baby.

It might not have been my actual birthday, but when the guys from the firehouse found me outside their door and rushed me to the hospital eleven years ago with sirens blaring, the doctor said it was as good a guess as any.

That's how I got August twenty-seventh.

When we let Parker inside, he's skittish around all the guys, with their big boots and heavy fireman's pants. He tucks his tail between his legs and his bones shake like it's the twenty-seventh of January. His wiry coat is brown except for two white patches, one over his left eye and one covering the tip of his tail as if he dipped it in paint. And his paws look too big for his body, like he might have more growing to do too.

Each guy takes a turn, saying, "It's *OK*. Here, boy." But the dog cowers and backs farther away from them the closer they get.

Not me, though. I get low and put my hand out slowly so he can smell. I look down his spine and count his ribs and watch him pull his ears back. His eyes are dark and scared. I rub my fingers together and just stay quiet like that until he moves one paw, and another, and then he walks up to me, parks his head on my left shoulder, and whimpers.

That's how I give him his name. Parker.

I was the same way, the guys tell me. When they heard my cries outside the firehouse door, they picked me up and brought me inside. I was skittish and scared and wouldn't stay parked on anyone's shoulder either. I wailed, red-faced, my little hands in tight fists. They say my cries were louder than the sirens of a five-alarm fire.

That's how they gave me my name. Cyrus.

Brooks, who likes to tell the others that he's been at that firehouse longer than they've been alive, said he wasn't one for holding babies and he'd pass. He held up his thick, calloused hands, shook his head, and pursed his lips to say no thanks. But they handed me to him anyway while they hopped in the truck and started the engine, and somewhere on his navy-blue firehouse T-shirt and suspender strap I found a place to be quiet and I slept there the whole ride as they tore through intersections all the way to the hospital.

As soon as Brooks handed me to the doctor, I started up again, crying and screaming, my gummy mouth open wide and my little chest heaving. They say the doctor tried all sorts of tricks to get me to calm down—different positions, a bottle of formula, a warm washcloth, a new diaper. But it wasn't until they handed me back to Brooks, my face on his T-shirt and suspender strap, that I stopped again and breathed.

The doctor took my temperature and squeezed my belly and looked in my ears and examined my skin, all while I was safe on Brooks's left shoulder. And I didn't cry again until he laid me down on the little plastic scale and the numbers popped up. Seven pounds, four ounces.

Through my siren cries, the doctor declared me healthy and lucky and said that he would take it from there.

The guys all sighed in relief and turned and slapped one another on the back, but when they noticed old Brooks wasn't with them they turned around. They could barely hear him through my red-faced wailing when he reached out and said to the doctor, "Maybe I should hold him just a little bit longer."

And that's how he became my dad.

When Parker puts his head on my left shoulder in the firehouse, the guys do the same thing they did on August twenty-seventh eleven years ago. They hop in the truck and start the engine, except this time they leave Leo behind to watch the potatoes boiling on the stove, they don't sound the sirens, and they drive the speed limit to the animal hospital instead of zooming through red lights to the emergency room.

They don't usually let me ride along in the truck. Instead, if there's an emergency while I'm there, I leave fast and walk up the street and over to my grandma's apartment in the assisted-living development, and I wait until my dad comes to pick me up. And that's fine by me, because I'm not brave like that. Brave like running-into-burning-buildings brave. Brave like my dad.

But when Mike claps me on the shoulder and says, "I think we're going to need you for this one," I climb right up in the truck and let Parker sit on my lap and stick his nose back on my shoulder. His hips are bony and dig into my thighs, but I don't let go of him the whole way.

When we get there, the vet examines him on a tall metal table, and Parker keeps his nose right beneath my ear, panting hot breath down my neck.

She peers in his eyes and squeezes his belly. "Malnourished."

I look up at my dad. "Hasn't eaten enough," he explains.

The vet parts his hair and examines his skin.

Parker yawns and whimpers and I hug him closer. My fingers fit in the grooves of his ribs the same way my dad taught me to slide my fingers between the laces of a football. But my hands feel more right where they belong holding Parker than they do around the leather of a ball.

"He'll stay here overnight," she says, massaging Parker's neck. "We'll scan for a microchip, try to find his owners, and hydrate and feed him slowly to see how he reacts."

Mike and Roger tuck their thumbs under the suspenders holding up their bulky fireman's pants, nod at the vet, say thank you, and turn their backs to leave.

"C'mon," my dad says and puts his arm around me.

But when I move my shoulder from under Parker's nose, he whines and claws at the metal table.

"Maybe I should hold him just a little longer?" I ask my dad.

But he shakes his head no. "They can take it from here."

Tears burn behind my eyes because it doesn't feel right to just leave him here. It's not where he belongs.

So I take off my T-shirt and give it a good rub against my skin, especially over my left shoulder and behind my ear, then put it down on the metal table and watch as he sniffs and sniffs, parks his nose into the fabric, and stops whimpering.

When I'm bare-chested like this, you can see my ribs too, but it's not because I'm malnourished. I definitely eat enough. I'm just built small. My dad assures me I'll fill out and be the best wide receiver in the league. I don't tell him that I don't want to be a wide receiver at all.

The vet smiles and my dad gives me his heavy canvas fireman's jacket. It reaches past my knees and is rough on my bare skin, but the weight of it feels good.

As we catch up with Mike and Roger outside, the vet comes through the front door.

"Before you go," she hollers, "is there a name you want us to call him?"

"Parker," I answer.

My dad looks down at me. His six feet four inches feel taller when I'm buried beneath his big jacket, the sleeves falling far below my hands even when I stretch my fingers straight out. He purses his lips and scrunches his brow into three big wrinkles. And I know what he's saying because I know my dad. He's saying I shouldn't give him a name, because we're not keeping him. He's not our dog.

On the drive back to the firehouse, the guys are laughing and joking and saying, "What is it about August twenty-seventh and our doorstep?" and I lean on my elbow out the fire truck window. It's getting dark and the air that finds its way through my dad's big jacket is cool against my skin, and I wonder how long Parker's been on his own, and I wonder if anyone is out there looking for him.

CHAPTER 2

Touch and Go

It's Dad's night to stay in the firehouse. I usually sleep on my grandma's pullout couch during his twenty-four-hour shifts, but it's my birthday and we always have my birthday dinner at the firehouse, plus it's Mike's last night before he retires, so Dad says I can stay with him in the bunks tonight. And even though I love my overnights with Grandma, the only other place I'd rather stay than the firehouse on my birthday is on the veterinarian's floor curled up with Parker, his nose on my left shoulder. And I know that's not going to happen.

When I sleep here, I'm on the top bunk right above Dad, and I'm locker number three, because besides Dad and Mike, I've been around the firehouse the longest. Roger joined the summer I turned five, and Leo was new last fall. After Mike retires, I'll move my stuff into locker number two, right next to Dad's.

My dad says even though he's older than Mike, there's no way he's going to retire any time soon. Not until he's old enough that he can't slide down the fireman's pole without busting his knees at the bottom, or until I'm old enough to take over locker number one. He says that this is right where he belongs.

I don't tell him that when he leaves the firehouse, I don't want to take over locker number one. That I want to leave with him and go do something else. That I love the firehouse when we're cooking dinner and hanging out around the table, or when we park on the street during Defeat of Jesse James Days and watch the botched bank robbery reenactment from the top of the truck, or when I'm holding Leo's feet on the gym mat while he does sit-ups, or if it's one of those times that Dad lets me stay for an overnight, when we eat popcorn and watch the Vikings game with our feet up.

But when the warning sirens blare and the guys start moving double time and speaking in code and the lights start flashing, then I don't like it anymore, and I'm happy to run to my grandma's apartment up the street, where it's quiet and safe. I don't tell him that I'm not brave like that. Brave like sliding-down-a-pole-and-landing-on-my-feet brave.

I run upstairs to the lockers, but before I can shake out of Dad's big jacket and pull on my own navy-blue fireman's T-shirt, I get an uneasy feeling in my belly because it doesn't really feel right, my grandma staying by herself on our usual sleepover days, even if my favorite nurse, Milly, is on tonight, and checks in extra on my grandma and fills up her candy dish with Werther's Originals when she's running low.

Ever since Grandma's stroke last year, things have been different. She can't move her right side the way she used to. Her foot drags when she walks, her arm stays tucked in tight to her side, her fist never opens, and her mouth droops a little, even when the rest of her is smiling.

And the worst of it all is that she can't talk. She tries and tries, but all that comes out are syllables. *Na na na na.* She points with her left hand and gets frustrated when I can't guess right and then just pinches her eyes closed tight and shakes her head like she's trying to tell me *Never mind* and *It's OK.* But she always opens her eyes and sees me there next to her and straightens up and smiles with her whole body. And then it feels good again, like that is right where I belong.

I pull on a T-shirt from my locker and head back downstairs. The guys are all clamoring in the kitchen to finish dinner. My dad is opening the cabinets and clanging pans, and Leo is mashing the potatoes, his muscles bulging with each smash. We have the same meal every August twenty-seventh—my special birthday meal.

Dad is pressing the ground beef into hamburger patties and Roger adds butter to the bowl of steaming potatoes.

"There's the birthday boy," Dad says.

"I still remember your first real meal with the guys, Cy . . ." Mike starts. This is the story he was telling a couple hours ago when we heard the whines at the front door, and it makes me wonder if Parker's had anything to eat yet.

Mike loves to tell this story every year on my birthday, and I think he loves it even more because Roger and Leo weren't there when it happened. They weren't part of the crew yet. "You should have seen it," he says to them. "Brooks came in with all these jars of baby food. Sloppy creamed spinach and mashed-up peas."

"That's what the book said to do," my dad interrupts. "Purees at six months."

"So on exactly February twenty-seventh," Mike continues, "Brooks opens these baby food jars and sits Cy right here on this very table and airplanes a spoon of green slop toward his lips. But Cy won't open."

My dad and Mike are laughing, and Leo says, "Smart

kid! I wouldn't open for green slop either!"

"Then Cy grabbed the spoon," my dad says, "and flung a green glob across the kitchen. But he still wouldn't open his mouth." His voice is gruff and matter-of-fact, and I like imagining him trying to feed little baby me with his big hand around a tiny spoon.

"Until we sat down with our burgers and mashed potatoes." Mike laughs.

I know this story by heart, and so do all the guys. They know that I cried and reached toward their dinner plates until Mike gave me a bite of his buttery, lumpy mashed potatoes, and my dad, who never gets loud or upset, grabbed a fistful of Mike's T-shirt and nearly punched his lights out because he thought I would choke. He kept shaking Mike and saying, "The book says purees!"

"No one had ever seen that side of your dad," Mike says. I smile because for some reason that feels like winning an MVP trophy.

I swallowed the potatoes just fine and kept pointing for more, more, until my dad gave in and I got another bite. Then another. And before the night was over I was eating bits of hamburger from between their fingers too.

"Cy was one of the guys from the beginning," Mike says. He starts scooping mashed potatoes on our plates, and Dad is sliding burgers onto buns.

We sit, all five of us, around the table, and Dad says the same thing he says every birthday dinner at the firehouse. "Thankful Cyrus cried at our door all those years ago."

And then Mike says the same thing he always says. "And may this August twenty-seventh be less eventful for Northfield, and its firemen." Everyone laughs, and Roger says something about "that dog showing up," and Mike says something about "not nearly as exciting as when Cy came."

"And here's to Mike's last night on the job," Dad adds.

We say cheers and clink our bottles of root beer and bite into our burgers. They're better off our grill in the backyard, but even here in the tiny firehouse kitchen, my dad makes the best burgers, and everyone agrees.

"When you retire, Brooks, you have to come back just to cook the burgers," Roger says.

"Don't be worrying about that any time soon." Dad runs his hand through his thick, graying hair.

I help myself to a second scoop of mashed potatoes, and Mike takes the ice cream out of the freezer to start thawing. This is another birthday tradition because what my dad still doesn't know is that after I ate potatoes and burger, when my dad turned his back to wash dishes, Mike spooned me my first bite of ice cream too.

When Mike told me that part of the story on my

seventh birthday, we agreed to let it be our little secret, because my dad, who wasn't one for babies and didn't know a thing about raising an infant, was following every word of this parenting book, and it said no sugar until one year. If he almost decked Mike over mashed potatoes, he definitely would have over chocolate ice cream.

Mike takes out five spoons and gives me a wink and a smile.

We scoop ice cream into mismatched mugs, and Roger sticks a candle in mine and lights a match. They sing "Happy Birthday," and I blow out the candle before the wax drips down to the chocolate.

"What a natural." Mike tousles my hair. "Firefighting is in your blood."

I smile, and I don't say that no one *actually* knows what's in my blood, but I know what he means. And I don't say that I didn't wish to be a fireman. I wished for Parker. I wished that the vet could get him to eat and drink and that Dad would soften the creases in his forehead and give up on his no-pet-no-way policy.

The guys disappear for a minute and come back out with two presents. One is wrapped in newspaper and duct tape, and the other is a plain white envelope. I already know what the first one is. A football. A junior size six, not the pee-wee ball we have at home, the one that Dad taught me how to throw a spiral with when I was five. I smile big even though I don't want it and I rip it open like I can't wait to put my fingers between the laces.

"This is a big year," Leo says.

And I know what he means. Sixth grade. Middle school. This is the first year I have tryouts, and this is the first year there isn't equal playing time, so the best kids on the team play the most. No one knows that I'm hoping I don't make the A Team because they have more practices, more games, and harder hits. No one knows that I hope I'm the last possible substitute on the very end of the B Team bench.

"This isn't Mighty-Mites anymore," Leo continues.

I want to tell him that it hasn't been Mighty-Mites since I turned ten last year. That was the year we stopped two-hand touch and started full tackle, the year I started faking fumbles to avoid hits.

"You've got to be ready for tomorrow." Leo pats me hard on the back.

The guys start chanting, "Olson! Olson!" And even though it's my last name too, I'm pretty sure they're cheering for my dad, who still holds the record for most touchdowns in a season at Joseph Lee Heywood Middle School and Northfield High School, and earned a starting spot at the University of Minnesota as a freshman.

Brooks Olson. Jersey number eighty-eight. Twenty-three touchdowns in his first season of middle school ball. A Team.

I join in the chanting too, until Dad tells us all to quit it and hands me the white envelope.

It's two tickets to a Minnesota Vikings game in October, and my jaw drops.

Mike, Roger, and Leo all raise their hands fast and start begging.

"You're going with *me*," Dad says.

I jump up and hug him, and I mean it, because I like *watching* football, especially with my dad. It gives me that same thrill as when we go see the sharks at the Mall of America aquarium. I could watch them swim for hours, as long as I'm on the other side of the glass. Same with football. I love watching the hard tackles and holding my breath for long throws, but only if I'm in the stands with a hot dog, or sitting on the firehouse couch next to Dad with my feet up.

"The seats are pretty close too," he says, pointing to the tickets. "So you can get some tips straight from the pros."

The guys laugh and say that my dad was practically pro, but he waves them off and says, "If any Olson is going pro, it's this one here." He ruffles my hair and that uneasy feeling turns in my stomach, but Dad's also looking at me with that half smile and squinty eyes. And I know my dad. He's saying he's proud of me.

"OK!" Leo says and claps his hands. "Time to get warmed up for tomorrow. Let's go, Olson!"

And this time, I know he's talking about me-Olson. He doesn't say anything else, just puts his mug in the sink and starts climbing the pole to the second floor without even using his legs. Roger follows him up the same way. I take the stairs, but I hustle, and Mike and my dad run up behind me.

Roger's at his locker changing into his ripped-sleeve workout tank, and Leo's doing jumping jacks on the gym mat. "Ready?" he huffs.

I shrug.

"First up, lunges." He shows me what they look like, lunging across the mat. A step, deep bend, knee barely touching the ground, and up. Step again, knee just barely touching, then up.

"Touch and go," he says. "Touch and go."

I ask if I can turn on some music, partly because it'll buy me a minute before I have to touch and go across the floor and partly because I like the way the old record player in the firehouse sounds, and I especially like the record I put on there yesterday, one I got from Grandma's apartment: *What'd I Say* by Ray Charles.

The record player is Mike's and has been at the

firehouse longer than I have, and I'm hoping he doesn't take it tomorrow when he leaves.

I lay the needle down in the groove, and the bass thrums. The piano and cymbals add in, and before I know it I'm trying to keep my foot from tapping, but my heart feels like it lifts right up with the notes and maybe I could do a hundred touch-and-goes. Yesterday, Grandma tapped her left foot along with the beat and sang *na, na* along with Ray Charles's *hey, heys* and her eyes were smiling watery, happy tears as the instruments blared, and before I left she pressed the record to my chest and said, "Na na." And I know my grandma. She was saying *It's yours.*

Leo snorts and says, "Someone must have changed the record. You can't work out to this."

The horns start and that's my favorite part and I want to tell Leo to keep his hands off that needle, but my words get stuck and my dad cuts in and says, "This is fine."

Mike nudges me onto the mat. There's a big mirror in front of us, and I look puny standing there next to Leo, who has muscles that you can see even when he's not flexing. When he steps, I follow. Step and lunge. I touch and go and touch and go, and try to keep up with the rhythm of the music, but after three, my legs are already burning and I want to stop.

"Take a knee," Dad says. "When you feel like it's too much, take a knee."

And I'm glad he says that, because the next touch I kneel and rest, and a rush of relief flows up my tired legs.

Then we switch to bench presses, and even though the trill of the trumpets gives me a boost of energy that I can feel down to the tips of my fingers, I still can't lift more than the bar's weight, and my arms start to tremble after five reps, and there's no taking a knee during bench presses, so Leo has to lift the bar off me.

I get a minute's rest, then Roger shows me how to hold a pair of dumbbells out from my sides and count. I only get to two before my whole body starts shaking. I can see my arms lowering and lowering in the mirror, until I give up and drop the dumbbells to the mat. My face is fire-engine red.

"That's enough for today," my dad says, and I'm really happy he does, because if it were up to Leo and Roger I think I'd be touching and going and pressing and lifting without breaks all the way until the sun comes up.

The guys slap me on the back and call me unstoppable and Roger lifts me up on his shoulders and they all start chanting, "Olson! Olson!" again and cheering for me like they did from the sideline of every Mighty-Mites game since first grade. And even though I have an uneasy feeling in my stomach and I wish I didn't have to go to tryouts tomorrow, all the guys rooting for me, with Ray Charles's hands dancing across the piano keys, feels pretty good.

That night, I take *What'd I Say* from the record player and slide it back in its sleeve. I can barely climb up to the top bunk because my legs are still wobbly from the three lunges and it's hard to raise my arms above my head. I lie on top of the wool blanket with the record pressed to my chest and think of Parker. I hope his nose is cold and still buried in my shirt, and I hope he's getting fluids and becoming stronger, and that tomorrow he won't shake and tremble like he did tonight. I hope the vet is staying over with him and he's not in some cage alone, and I hope there's music playing, and I hope she checks in on him extra and gives him treats and scratches him behind the ears.

And I'm wondering if his owner just let him run off the leash too fast and too far, and if he's out there searching and searching and calling out Parker's real name. Or maybe he couldn't take care of him anymore, so he had to leave him, let him wander off on his own. Maybe Parker's been all alone getting skinny and scared, and his owner's at home worrying and hoping someone else has taken him in and made him family.

I fall asleep imagining his nose parked right there on my left shoulder, his hot breath down my neck.

CHAPTER 3

Tryouts

In the morning, I lower my sore body down from the top bunk, put the Ray Charles record in my locker, then shake my dad awake.

"Let's call the vet," I say.

He rolls over and grumbles. "I bet they're not open yet."

"Try." I hand him his cell phone.

He sits up and rubs his eyes. "Fine."

Someone picks up right away, and my dad clears his throat and says we were in last night with a dog. A stray. He listens and waits and says, "I see," then, "Thanks again. Will do." And hangs up.

"So?" I ask.

"She'll update us later. He's still touch and go."

I just keep looking at him because I don't know what that means.

"They're not sure if he's recovering yet," he says. "Still have to see. Touch and go."

My stomach sinks and turns.

"We should visit . . ." I start.

But Dad looks right at me and pinches his lips together, and I know my dad. He's saying that we can't. It'll just make things harder, and he really is sorry. "Let the vet do her job," he says. "We'll call again tomorrow."

I lie back on his bunk and close my eyes and try not to think about Parker, and how I hope he can last in touch-and-go longer than I can.

"Plus," Dad says, "it's your big day."

As soon as we step out of the car at Joseph Lee Heywood Middle School, the coach calls out, "Well, if it isn't Brooks Olson!" He's jogging toward us, waving his clipboard, his whistle bouncing. I'm wondering if he can see from there that I'm not too much like my dad, who has wide shoulders and big hands. My shoulders don't fill out a youth small T-shirt, and my hands can hardly grip a junior size-six football.

We're early, but I can see Marcus and Shane tossing a ball back and forth on the field, and that uneasy feeling in my stomach settles down a little because tryouts would stink even more if I didn't know anyone.

A few older kids are stretching and lacing up their cleats on the bench, and they look over too. One of them points and I can hear him say, "Twenty-three touchdowns!" My dad pretends not to notice.

Marcus tosses the ball to Shane and looks up. He waves at me and I wave back, but I can't run over there because the coach is just getting to the parking lot to meet us and giving my dad a friendly punch on the shoulder. He hands him a playbook. "Thought you might like to glance at this."

My dad nods and says he'll look it over.

Then the coach looks down at me. "And this must be our next wide-receiving star!"

Dad pats my brown curls, which are still fuzzy from sleeping, and says, "That's right."

I stick out my hand to shake because that's what Dad taught me to do. I tell him my name is Cyrus, but I don't tell him I'm not a star at much—not touch-and-goes, not bench presses, and definitely not wide receiving. And that's just football.

I'm not a star at most everything else too.

No one knows that, except for the pictures, I can't even read two pages of that playbook and keep the words in my brain long enough to understand them all together.

Because that's a secret, and I guess I'm actually kind of a star at keeping it that way. I made it all the way to the sixth grade without anyone finding out.

"Happy to meet you," he says, and he calls me Olson. "I'm Coach Matthews." His handshake is tight.

Marcus and Shane are calling my name from the field and waving me over. I look up at my dad, and I almost say *Can we please get back in the car and forget about football and drive to the animal hospital to check on Parker instead?* But my dad is smiling down at me, and before any words can come out, my throat closes up and he says, "Go on." He pats my back and says, "You got this. I'll be back in an hour."

I head toward Marcus and Shane, my bag bouncing against my leg as I jog, and when I look back at my dad, he runs his hands through his hair, gives me a thumbs-up, and yells, "Have fun!" I send him a thumbs-up back but really I'm wishing the hour were already over and that Coach Matthews would call and say he was sorry to report that I didn't make the A Team.

When I get to Marcus and Shane they stick out their fists for bumps and say, "What's up?" and "Happy belated birthday," but I can tell that they're nervous. Probably because they started liking football even more when we switched to full tackle last year, and they actually want to make the A Team. They sit next to me on the grass while I pull on my cleats.

"You're so lucky the coach knows your dad," Shane says.

"Everyone knows Cy's dad," says Marcus.

"Yeah, well, I hope the coach doesn't expect me to have that Olson gene, because I don't."

That's the actual truth, and it's pretty easy to tell.

"You're totally going to make the A Team," Shane says.

I hope not, I'm thinking.

"We all are," Marcus adds. "Plus, Cy, you're due for a good season. Last year was rough."

I nod and say, "No kidding," and start lacing up my cleats, which never feel right on my feet. They pinch my pinkie toes, even if I tie them loose, and the left one slips on my heel and rubs a sore spot that sometimes bleeds into my sock. It's not the cleats. This is my third pair. My feet just aren't built for football. But after returning the first two pairs, and having three different salesmen measure my feet and study my arches, I finally just told my dad that these ones fit like a charm.

He put his arm around my shoulders in the store. "Should have known," he said. "You're a Nike Vapor Ultrafly kid."

I didn't know how to tell him that I didn't feel ultra-fly, not at all, especially with my pinkies pinched in like this, so we just bought the cleats and took them home and started breaking them in with long passes in the backyard.

"Sweet cleats," Marcus says, and runs his finger over the black Nike swoosh on my right foot.

"They're all right," I answer.

Shane stands and pulls his right leg behind him to stretch, and he doesn't waver or fall over or anything. I do all my stretches sitting. I stay down in the grass with my legs out and try to touch my toes but only get halfway down my shins. I pull one arm across my chest, then the other. Even though that stretch never feels like anything, everyone always does it, so I fake that I'm getting good and limber and ready.

"Go long," Marcus says. He pulls a ball behind his head and juts his chin down the field. Shane cheers me on, and I get up and start running. I like this part. Just the three of us, out on the field, running routes and throwing long passes, spiking touchdowns and doing silly end-zone dances like we're seven years old again. Like any time before last year.

The three of us have been friends since pre-K when Shane and I were in Ms. Hendricks's class together. I met

Marcus that same year, when he and his mom walked over to the firehouse to say that their cat was stuck up a tree. My dad said I could come for that one, so we rode in the truck to Marcus's house, and sure enough, there was Harry, their shaggy black cat, out on a thick limb of their backyard tree. He had gotten too close to a nest of blue jays, and the mommy bird was dive-bombing Harry, beak first, trying to protect her babies.

I remember feeling bad for poor old Harry, but also thinking that the bird was just being a good mom.

We were all in Mr. Garrison's class for kindergarten, and that's when we started tossing a pee-wee-sized football in our backyards after school. Then we joined the Mighty-Mites together, and we've been friends ever since.

I look back, and Marcus juts his chin and wags his hand, and I know what he's saying: *Look left, zag right, hand out, touchdown!* Because I know Marcus, and he's good at making calls.

I follow his commands and fake right around a pretend defender and catch the ball easily and run it across the end zone for a spike.

"Touchdown!" Marcus yells. "Where were those steady hands last year?" He says it like a joke, but I know he's seriously ready for me to get over my fifth-grade fumbles so he can put up good numbers this year. "If the old Olson is back, then we've got this," he says.

But as we walk toward the bench where all the seventh and eighth graders are lacing up their cleats and smudging eye black on their cheeks, what I'm really wishing is that I could zag left and fake right and run right back to the firehouse.

Coach Matthews blows his whistle, then yells, "Huddle up!"

"This is it," Marcus says.

"Ready?" asks Shane.

I don't say no, but no.

Coach Matthews is standing up on the first bleacher and we're all gathered around beneath him. He waves his arms when he talks, the papers on his clipboard blowing in the breeze.

"Who here knows who your middle school is named for?" He pauses, and every single one of us raises our hand, because if you grew up in Northfield, or have been here for more than a day, you know who Joseph Lee Heywood was. He was the guy who refused to open the safe and kept Jesse James from robbing the bank in town a million years ago.

"This town is famous for its bravery, for blocking the bad guys. We have a long tradition of courage here in

Northfield!" He pauses again and takes a deep breath, and his face is getting a little red because he's kind of shouting.

"You are here to try out for the Heywood football team!" He's pointing his finger and getting louder. "Today you will work harder than you ever thought possible! You will give one hundred and ten percent! You will leave here sore and praying that you make the cut so you can return tomorrow to work even harder!" Then he stops and gazes out over all of us. "If you think you are in the wrong place, raise your hand now."

A few kids laugh, but the coach keeps looking at each one of us like he's completely serious and this is our last chance to bail. And when his eyes reach me, I wonder if he can see through the Vikings jersey my dad surprised me with this morning, right through the too-big shoulder pads that reach down over my chest, and straight through to my heart, and I wonder if he can see that this is not where I belong.

But he smiles at me and nods, and his eyes move on.

"OK then," he shouts. "Let's play!"

Coach Matthews wasn't kidding when he said 110 percent. I have to give that much just to get to the first water break fifteen minutes in, and all we've done is warm up. We ran a lap around the field in our pads and then lined up in rows to do jumping jacks and high knees and all these other things that made me sweat into my eyes.

I'm squirting water from my bottle through my face mask, and even though it looks easy when I see the Vikings players do it on TV, I still get it all over my face and it drips down my neck and into my jersey, which actually feels pretty good because it's also 110 degrees under these pads.

Shane takes a gulp of yellow Gatorade. "The eighth graders are big."

And if Shane is saying that, you know it's true, because he's five feet four inches and maybe even that wide across too. His shoulders are broad, and his jersey fits tight over his stomach and chest, and his legs are round and sturdy like fire hydrants, and just by looking at him you know his position. Offensive center. He snaps the ball, then shields the quarterback and plows into people and makes everyone scared when they're lined up nose to nose.

"The eighth graders aren't just big, they're huge." Marcus spits his neon green mouth guard into his hand and shoves an orange slice in. Someone's mom brought a big Tupperware full of them to share.

Marcus is a quarterback. Shane's been protecting him since we were seven, and I've been running long and catching his passes before the defenders could lay two hands on me.

I'm a wide receiver. That's what my dad was. I have pretty good speed, and I know the game because I never miss watching the Vikings. I know how to run a route and follow a play. I know how to cut and weave and lose a defender. I just don't do it anymore, because if I get the ball, then all eyes are on me, and guys who are a foot taller and three feet wider will be hustling to smash me to the ground, and if the ball pops loose, then they'll run full speed and jump, and I'll be breaking my bones at the bottom of a pile of knees and cleats and helmets and sweaty tight-bellied jerseys. And I'm not brave like that. Brave like break-my-bones-for-the-love-of-the-game kind of brave.

I take off my helmet so I can get a real sip of water, and I pop in an orange slice too. It tastes so good, and if football were all huddles and halftime breaks, talking about the game and the plays, and eating fruit, I'd probably be MVP.

Coach Matthews is blowing on his whistle already and hollering that defense will go with Coach Thompson and offense will come with him.

I put my helmet back on, and all the offensive players watch as Coach Matthews scribbles some routes on his clipboard, and before I can sink my teeth back into the new mouth guard that I dropped in boiling water and molded to my jaw last week, he's saying, "Olson! Show them how it's done!"

"Me?" I sputter.

"You."

"Assistant Coach Erikson will play cornerback, and . . ." He scans the crowd of us. "You!" He points to Marcus. "You ready to throw? Let's see how tough the sixth graders are this year."

Marcus hurries to the line and does that arm stretch across his chest that doesn't work for me and hops up and down on his unpinched toes.

"Ready!" he shouts.

Coach Matthews tosses the ball to Shane. "Snap?"

Shane nods his head and lines up. He snaps the ball back to Marcus, and I'm off, running the route the way I've practiced over and over in our backyards. It wouldn't be hard to fake a cut and lose Assistant Coach Erikson and receive Marcus's pass. Coaches never go one hundred percent. And even if I couldn't get away from him, I'm pretty sure that coaches can't tackle kids anyway. I think that might be illegal. At least, I figure, he wouldn't hit hard.

I don't want to catch Marcus's pass, though. Because I don't want to make the A Team, and I wish it were possible to not make the B Team. Because I don't want to be chased and tackled all season.

But I also don't want to make Marcus look bad, because he *does* want to make the A Team, and I think he's good enough to, even if the eighth graders are huge.

So I cut loose and raise my right hand, calling for the ball, running toward the end zone. Marcus pulls his arm back, locks his eyes with mine, and sends a perfect spiral right to my open hand. It hits my palm, bull's-eye.

I could wrap my fingers around it and pull it to my chest like my dad taught me, but instead I bobble it back and forth between right and left and right again, then drop it.

All the other kids groan and say, "Noooooo," and look away like it's the ugliest thing they've ever seen.

Marcus slaps his hand against his thigh and shakes his head. "What the heck, Cyrus?"

"Perfect throw!" I shout, making sure Coach Matthews can hear. "It was perfect! I just have butterfingers!"

I hang my head and run back to the rest of the group.

Three other kids run the same route, and Marcus hits their hands just as perfectly. Two out of the three catch it, and run it to the end zone for a spike. The one that misses really misses, a right-through-the-hands kind of miss, and I don't think he's trying to either, because he rips his helmet off and throws it to the ground and says a couple words that make Assistant Coach Erikson say, "Hey, hey, now."

Coach Matthews pats Marcus's shoulder pads and says, "Well done," and calls up another quarterback to try.

I don't want a second turn, so I ask the coaches if I can go to the bathroom, and I'm actually pretty good at faking that I really have to go because it's the best move I have during English class too. As soon as the teacher wants us to read something, then partner up to discuss it, that's when I raise my hand, right when we're supposed to talk about what we read. I give a little jiggly dance and say it's an emergency.

"Quick," Coach Matthews says and points toward big blue double doors on the side of the middle school building. I run off fast, past all the other preseason tryouts—soccer and field hockey—and I'm wondering if everyone really wants to be kicking balls and whacking sticks with a whole opposing team chasing after them, or if I'm the only faker out here.

The bathroom is at the end of the hall. All the lights are turned off and the lockers are open and empty and everything smells like the cleaning products they use at the doctors' office. It's weird to be in a school before the year starts, and I think about how next week this hallway will be filled with a hundred kids.

Last year, we had cubbies in our classrooms, but now we'll be switching rooms and teachers for every subject, so we'll get tall, red lockers that line the hallway and slam and have combination lock codes that we'll have to remember.

I pass by a couple classrooms and search for signs with the teachers' names to see if I recognize any from the schedule that was mailed home at the end of fifth grade. One door is decorated with a dozen book covers printed off in color, and right in the middle of the door it says *Mr. Hewett, 6th Grade English*. I remember his name.

I peek in the window, and I can't see much. All the tables and chairs are stacked and pushed to one side, and there are shelves that wrap the whole way around the room. Each shelf is packed with baskets that are full of books. There's a whole library right there in the classroom.

I look at the walls and the whiteboard and try to find any clues about what books we might be reading this year so I can get started looking up summaries online and memorize a couple themes to write about in my journal, but I can't tell.

I lean in close and see a huge bulletin board covered with blue paper, and on the top it says *Classroom Book a Day*. I can read it because it's not words I can't read.

I can sound out almost any word, even really long ones, and read perfectly for a hundred chapters, but when I have to string them all together and tell you what I read, that's when my brain goes blank and I can't remember any of the words or how they fit together. It's easier when someone reads out loud and I can just focus on listening to the story, but I'm hoping Mr. Hewett doesn't think I can read a book a day by myself when I haven't even really ever read one.

Coach's whistle screams from the field, and I better move it, but as I'm hustling out I see the trophy case and an old picture of my dad in his jersey—number eighty-eight. His name is engraved on a plaque that says *Football Records* and *23 Touchdowns*.

It's weird to think of Dad at my age, and to see his picture in my new middle school and imagine him walking down the hall to class. And I bet when I get to high school it'll be the same thing, because he holds records there too.

I smile at his picture, then the whistle screams again, so I run with my pinchy cleats clicking down on the freshly waxed floor and out the blue doors and back to the field.

At the end of practice, Coach Matthews lines us all up in the end zone to run. Line touches, he calls them. "You run to the line, touch it, and run back. Touch the line, run to the next one." He's pointing down the field. "Touch. Go. Touch. Go. Got it?"

It makes me think of lunges and Parker, and now I can't stop wondering if he's OK and if he has a big pen or a little cage and if he's getting along with the other dogs and if he's gotten any bones. I wonder if he still has my T-shirt, and if he remembers me.

The whistle blows, and I get a late start on purpose. I'm still touching while everyone else is going. Then I see my dad's Volvo station wagon pull into the parking lot, and even if my legs burn and I want to finish in the back of the pack, I pick up the pace and pass a few of the other guys who started out too fast and are losing steam.

My dad leans on the hood of the car and shields his eyes from the sun as I pass two more guys. Through my face mask, I can see his lips press into a little half smile.

When the whistle blows for us to stop, I'm in the middle of the pack, finishing with Shane, who is huffing and heaving. It's ahead of where I wanted to finish, but I'm still not a star. Not like Marcus, who was neck and neck with the eighth graders out front.

Coach calls us all together for a final huddle. "There are forty-four of you here today." He's standing up on the first bleacher and we're all still breathing hard. "I will see thirty of you back here tomorrow to continue your fight for a spot on the A Team. The rest of you will play B Team ball this season. You'll hear from us this afternoon."

Shane, Marcus, and I sit on the bench and loosen our cleats. We take off our pads and pack up our bags. I'm too tired to talk, and I think they are too, because they don't say anything about my missed pass.

When we're halfway to the parking lot, Coach Matthews calls me back. "Olson!" He's standing with the other coaches and waving me over with his clipboard.

Shane and Marcus give me worried looks, but they stick their fists out for bumps and Marcus says, "Call you later, when I hear from the coach."

"OK," I say. But I'm really thinking that maybe the coaches can't even wait until this afternoon to tell me I didn't make the cut. That I was that bad.

I jog back on wobbly legs and instead of putting a disappointed hand on my shoulder, Coach Matthews hands me a pair of Under Armour gloves still in the plastic packaging. "We have a few extra. Every star wide receiver has to have a good pair of gloves."

"No more butterfingers," Assistant Coach Erikson says.

I nod and say thanks and that maybe these will help.

"You got this, Olson." They clap me on the back, and I jog to the parking lot.

In the car, I unwrap the gloves and try them on. They're a little big, but I pull the Velcro tight around my wrists.

My dad reaches over. "Sticky palms to help you grip the ball."

"Cool," I say. But really I'm thinking that for me, playing football just doesn't stick. And beneath the pads and pinched into the cleats with sticky gloves cinched tight around my wrists is not where I belong.

CHAPTER 4

Olson Gene

On the way home, we stop at Grandma's apartment. She lives in a development with a lot of other grandmas and grandpas and there are a bunch of nurses who all know my name, and a big dining room where all the residents get served like they're in a restaurant for every meal. The lobby has comfortable couches, rocking chairs, and a big fireplace. There's also a shiny grand piano, and it's my favorite when someone is playing. It makes me walk down the hall to Grandma's apartment a whole different way, like the music is in my body and making my feet step right on beat until I get to her door, apartment number five on the first floor.

Someone is playing today, an Elton John song I know from when Grandma used to play her old yellow-painted upright piano and sing to me, but my toes are aching from being squished in my Nike Vapor Ultraflies, and it's throwing me off and making it hard to walk on beat the way I like to.

Milly is coming out of my grandma's room as we're going in.

"Look who it is!" she says. "The birthday boy!" She wears a stethoscope around her neck and shakes a bottle of pills like it's a party instrument, moving her hips in a quick little dance, like maybe she has music in her body too.

I smile. "It was yesterday."

"Oh, no, no." She wags her finger at me. "You get the whole week to celebrate, especially when you turn an important age like eleven." She gives me a big hug even though I'm still a little sweaty from touch-and-goes, and the streaks of eye black that Shane swiped on my cheeks before tryouts smudge a little on her nurse's smock right next to her name tag.

Milly has long, wavy black hair that's always pulled back tight and the widest smile I've ever seen, and when she talks, her voice sounds different from any other voices I've heard, like it matches the music in her body and always comes out on rhythm. Hugging her is like falling into pillows, and she doesn't let go fast either, like most people. She wraps her arms right around and holds on tight like she really means it, and every time I know exactly what she's thinking: that she's really happy to see me. And that feels good.

She puts her hand on my dad's shoulder and says, "*Hola*," and asks him how he feels to be the dad of a boy who's eleven now.

"Old," he replies. "I'm going to need a room here myself pretty soon." They both chuckle.

Then Milly opens Grandma's door and peeks her head in. "Anita Bonita, you have two very handsome visitors," she calls.

I hear my grandma inside. "Na na na na!"

"Oh, you just wait and see, Anita," Milly says. "Even more handsome than the ones you had earlier!"

Grandma laughs, and that makes me like Milly even more because she's quick with jokes and always knows the right things to say. And even if so much else has changed, Grandma's laugh sounds just like it always has my whole life, deep and low and so uncontrollable that it makes tears squeeze from the corners of her eyes.

Milly pats me on my back and calls me *muchacho*, then knocks on the lady's door across the hall and enters with that same sweet voice she uses with my grandma.

"Hi, Mom," Dad says as we go in. He leans down to kiss her on the cheek, but she waves him away.

"Na na na." She's pushing my dad to the side with

her left arm and waving me over.

This is one of our things. She ignores him and pretends she's only excited to see me, like I'm the very best thing about my dad. Then she pulls me in close with a hug that used to feel like Milly's hugs, big and pillowy and tight, but now she can only do it from one side. And even though I'm not built big like my dad, or pillowy like Milly and Grandma, I make sure to reach both my arms all the way around her to complete the circle.

She used to say, "To heck with you, Brooks, how's my only grandson?" And she still says that, but now she says it with her face and her body and the way she changes her voice for each *na na na*.

"I'm good, Grandma."

She makes a big deal out of my new Vikings jersey and cleats and the smudged eye black on my cheeks. Grandma came to all my Mighty-Mites games. She would sit with the guys from the firehouse and jump up to cheer and sometimes to yell at the referee. But since her stroke she hasn't come to any games, which is OK with me because that was last year, right when we switched from two-hand touch to full tackle, and Grandma is too smart to chalk up all that fumbling to a growth spurt, like my dad does, or a bad season, like Marcus and Shane do.

She didn't just stop going to my games, though, she

stopped going anywhere. Dad says she's too proud and doesn't want to be pushed in a wheelchair or dragging her right side and *na na na*–ing.

She kisses me a hundred times on my cheek and doesn't let go of my hand until she points to her record collection, skinny spines packed into the shelves that cover a whole wall. And I know what she's saying because I know my grandma. She's saying *Pick a record*. This is another one of our things. I run my fingers across the spines and pull one out without looking at the cover. She used to smile and laugh and take the record from me and tell me a long story about the first time she saw this artist or that band, or how she used to dance to this one with my grandpa when he was alive. Then I'd stay until we listened to every song.

Now when I pull a record and show her the cover, she puts her left hand on her heart and closes her eyes, and I put it on the player and lower the needle. And now when I leave, she presses the record to my chest and says, "Na na." *It's yours.*

Today I pull out Smokey Robinson and the Miracles' *Going to a Go-Go*, and Grandma puts her hand to her heart, and before I even drop the needle in the groove she's swaying back and forth in her chair. Then I sit down and she reaches over and grabs my hand and squeezes it tight, right on beat.

When Grandma had her stroke, the guys from the firehouse helped Dad and me move all her furniture from her old house, the one Dad grew up in on the Carleton College campus right in town, to this apartment at the assisted-living home. We carried her couch, recliner chair, coffee table, bed frame and mattress, nightstand, and boxes of her clothes. We lugged her shelves and all her records because she wouldn't let us leave even one behind, and we tried to make the tiny one-bedroom apartment look as much like the old house on College Street as we could.

When we first brought her in, she stood up from her wheelchair even though she wasn't supposed to, put all her weight on her one good leg, and said, "Na na!" over and over and pointed to the couch and chair. Milly told us it was normal for residents to resist their new homes and become agitated, but I know my grandma, and I knew that wasn't it. She wanted something, and she wasn't going to give up until we understood.

She pointed and pointed and *na na na*—ed until tears ran from her eyes, and I finally got it. "You want us to switch the couch and your chair?" I asked.

She pumped her left fist and pulled me in around my neck and kissed and kissed my cheeks. "Na na na!"

So my dad and Mike switched the furniture while

she waited, even though that's not how it was set up in the house on College Street. Then Dad helped her into the recliner where she always sat and she demanded I sit down on the couch next to her.

With the furniture this way, she could reach out her left arm out and hold my hand. That's what she wanted.

And that's exactly what she did. She held on to me with her one good hand and put her head back and closed her eyes, tears still squeezing from the edges, and she smiled a half smile from the left side of her face. Then she fell asleep. And even if this place didn't feel like home yet, or maybe it never would feel like my grandma's home on College Street, at least I knew that at my grandma's left side was right where I belonged.

Now Grandma's pointing to two small packages on the coffee table. I can tell she wrapped them herself because there's no tape and the paper is crinkled and squeezed and folded over, and even if I hadn't seen the ragged wrap job, I'd still know she did it herself with her left hand because that's my grandma. She's not a big fan of help.

"Grandma, you didn't have to get me—"

"Na na!" she says and points again.

I pick up the smaller one and the paper starts unfolding on its own. Inside is a square plastic case, and inside that is a chain necklace with two tags. Punched into the aluminum is *Thomas B. Olson* and a bunch of numbers and letters.

"Na na na na," Grandma says. She puts out her hand, and I lay the tags in her palm. She runs her thumb over *Thomas B. Olson* and closes her eyes and kisses the tags and hands them back.

I look at my dad. "Your great-grandpa's World War II identification." He tells me that my grandpa, who died of cancer before I showed up wailing at the firehouse steps, wore these every day, and Grandma's been holding on to them for me.

Then he points to the tags and explains what everything stands for. His army ID number. *P* for Protestant. *O* for blood type.

Knowing that these were on my great-grandpa's chest, below his uniform, while he was fighting the Nazis makes them feel heavier and more important and like maybe I shouldn't be the one putting them around my neck now. But when I do, Grandma squeezes my hand, and I know my grandma, and I know what she's saying. *They're yours now, and they're right where they belong.*

I glance up at my dad because I feel like they should be around his neck instead, but he looks down at me with the same eyes Grandma has. He's saying that it's OK, and he has enough from Thomas B. Olson, like six feet four inches, and thick, straight silvery hair, and that brave Olson gene.

I reach over and hug Grandma, and she pats my head and kisses my cheek and points at the other present.

I already know this one is a book, and I'm already nervous to open it because then I'll have to pretend I like it and pretend to read it, and it feels bad to pretend to Grandma.

The paper falls off, and I see a one-eyed face on a blue cover. *Wonder* by R.J. Palacio. I take a deep breath of relief because even though there are too many words on each page and too many pages for me to keep straight, I've seen this book before and I know there's a movie of it now, so I'll be able to tell Grandma what happens in the story and how much I love it.

I pass it to my dad so he can look, and I give Grandma another big hug, and right then there's a knock on the door and Milly comes in with three square pieces of chocolate cake on paper plates from the kitchen. Eleven skinny candles stick out of the biggest piece. "Whoever said you can't have cake before lunch?" she jokes.

Instead of singing "Happy birthday," Grandma starts *na na na*–ing to the song Smokey Robinson is singing, and she's right on tune. She dances with her shoulders and leans toward me and Smokey is singing about "All That's Good." She's saying she loves me and that *I'm* all that's good, and when the horns start climbing up and up I can feel the music deep down in, right down to where Grandma loves me.

Milly is dancing with the cake slices, and even Dad, who isn't one for singing, joins in and hums and tousles my hair and says, "Lucky you. Another birthday wish."

Milly sets the plates down on the coffee table next to *Wonder*, and I take a big breath in and think about Parker, and I'm betting that if I wish twice for the same thing it'll have a better chance of coming true. So I wish and I wish and I wish for the same thing I wished for last night at the firehouse: that Parker's not skittish and scared anymore and that he finds a good family fast.

I would wish that my dad would let us go visit and take him for a walk and bring him a bone, so he could see that Parker belongs with me. But I know my dad, and I know he won't change his *no* into a *yes*, or even into a *maybe*, and I don't want to waste my wish.

I blow out the candles and everyone cheers. Grandma unfolds a tray from the side of her chair, and Milly lays out three forks and napkins on the coffee table. Dad stands and tries to help Grandma with her fork, but she pulls her arm away fast and scowls.

"Oh, Brooks, you know better than to help Anita," Milly says and winks at Grandma. "She's better with her left hand than I am with my right!" That makes

Grandma laugh, and Milly smiles and says to enjoy the cake and don't I dare try leaving without saying good-bye. I nod and say OK, and before Milly goes she quick tucks a napkin into the neck of my grandma's shirt and turns fast to leave like it's no big deal. My grandma rolls her eyes, but she doesn't yank the napkin out.

I'm not expecting the cake to be good because it's made for old people and probably has no sugar, but it's actually not bad and I eat it fast and I could probably even eat another piece.

"Cy is going through quite the growth spurt," Dad says, looking down at the crumbs on my plate. I want to tell him that it's not a growth spurt. I'm still four feet eight inches.

Grandma stabs at her cake with the fork in her left hand, then balances it and quickly brings it to her mouth. Every once in a while the cake doesn't make it all the way and a bite falls down her napkin, swipes her shirt, and lands back on the tray.

"Na!" she grunts, and I know what she's saying. She's saying *Damn* because that's a word she used to say all the time. Then she'd say *damn* again when she realized she'd said *damn* in front of me, and that got us laughing every time.

She shakes her head and tries to wipe the chocolate off her shirt.

"It's OK, Mom," my dad says, and he uses his napkin to dab the chocolate.

She pushes him off hard and shakes her head no, and my dad takes his napkin back and says he's going to the bathroom. And even though he never gets mad, I can tell he's a little frustrated. I guess if your whole life is rescuing kids from windows and cats from trees, you probably want to take care of your own mom too. But like Milly said, Grandma's not a big fan of help.

When Dad's in the bathroom, she reaches over and pinches my jersey again and asks, "Na na?"

"Yeah, we had tryouts today." I try not to make a big deal of it, because I don't want her to feel bad for me when I don't make the A Team.

"Na na na . . ." She wants to know how it went.

"It was OK."

She raises her eyebrows like she knows. Like she knows I'm done with playing football. Like she knows I don't care one bit about making any team.

"Na na," she says and squeezes my hand again. And I know she's saying *You'll figure this out.*

I smile and thumb through *Wonder*, which is even longer than I thought and doesn't have any pictures to help. The words on the pages fly by and by, and I don't have any idea how anyone keeps them all in one brain while they read.

Then Grandma squeezes my hand again and nods toward the book like she's saying *And you'll figure this out too.* And I'm pretty sure my grandma knows everything that's deep in me, and that my secrets are safe with her.

I slide Smokey Robinson back in its sleeve, and Grandma says, "Na na," and presses it to my chest. *It's yours.*

When Dad gets back from the bathroom, Grandma's eyes look tired and it's time to let her rest. I hug her tight and my great-grandpa Olson's dog tags drape between us. She rubs them between her thumb and finger again and pinches my cheek right below the smudged eye black.

And even though I never met him, I'm glad I got something from my great-grandpa Olson because it isn't looking like I'm going to get his six feet four inches, and I definitely don't have that Olson gene that turns them into war heroes and firefighting football stars. I'm just not brave like that. Wear-my-blood-type-around-my-neck brave.

When we get home, I kick off my cleats and wiggle my toes. I'm just starting to feel further away and free from touch-and-goes and long passes and plasticky-tasting mouth guards when Dad presses his cell phone against my ear and says, "Listen." It's a voice mail from Coach

Matthews. I made the first cut. He'll see me again tomorrow at tryouts.

My dad is smiling big, so I do too, but I get that uneasy feeling in my stomach. When he lowers the phone, I see there's another voice mail from an unknown number, and I'm thinking about Parker. I look up at Dad and raise my eyebrows, and he nods and pushes speaker.

"This message is for Brooks and Cyrus." I get closer to the phone as if I could feel Parker's hot breath right through it.

She says that Parker was touch and go all morning but that he's eating and drinking now, off all IVs, and has been treated for heartworm and given a bath. "No microchip. We're moving him to the humane society first thing tomorrow."

I look up at Dad because I don't know what that is.

"Humane. They'll be nice to him." He puts his big hand on my shoulder. "They'll find him a family."

He moves his hand to the back of my neck and looks down at me. He's saying that's it, that's all we can do, nothing more to talk about. But I'm staring at the phone and hoping it rings right now and it's the veterinarian calling back to say she thinks it might be best if we come visit and try him out at our home just for a little while. But the phone stays silent.

"Can we call her back and ask if he's wagged his

tail?" I ask. Dad shakes his head.

"Shouldn't we at least go check in so he knows we didn't forget about him?"

He shakes his head again. "No sense in getting attached."

"But . . ."

He looks down at me and I know he means it. He's telling me to stay clear of the humane society, and not to let Parker rest his head on my shoulder, because he's not our dog and he's not going to be our dog. And I wonder if that's what happened with me eleven years ago. He held me one second too long, and then he couldn't let go.

CHAPTER 5

Huh Huh Graaa

There are thirty of us at tryouts today. Fourteen kids were cut to the B Team, and only five sixth graders are still here. I can't believe I'm one of them. I don't think Marcus and Shane can really believe it either.

"You've got to catch something today, Olson," Marcus says.

I nod, then Coach Matthews shouts, "Ready?" and blows his whistle.

Marcus and Shane chant, "One, two, three," and jump up and crash their chests into each other and then grunt a bunch of syllables that sound like *huh gra huh huh huh graaaaa!* I might have started tripping and fumbling more last year, but as soon as we switched to full tackle, they got more aggressive and tougher, and I'm pretty sure they actually did go through growth spurts.

My hands are sweating in the new sticky wide receiver gloves, and I know Coach Matthews is expecting me to make a big catch too. I feel bad that he wasted his new gloves on me, but maybe I'll give them back when I don't make the cut and some other kid who's bigger and stronger and more brave than I am will get the ball to stick to them every time.

Everyone is standing around, stretching their legs. I'm too sore to even think about bending over to touch my pinchy cleats. I didn't have enough time to get unsore from touch-and-goes in the firehouse with the guys before I got sore again yesterday from tryouts, so now I'm sore on top of sore.

"We've made it this far," Marcus says. "Today we have to give it everything."

He even talks like a pro, pumping up his team as if he's at the center of the stadium with seventy-three thousand people staring down at him.

Marcus has always been the quarterback of our trio. He makes the calls, and Shane defends him, even if it's to try anchovies on pizza when everyone knows that's a terrible idea. They've been my friends forever, but I sometimes feel like I'm running out on my own and looking back with my hands up, tracking some throw that I'm not sure I really want to catch.

Coach Matthews lines us up, and before I can play with the laces on my cleats to give my toes more wiggle room, we're clamping down on our mouth guards and running in place.

"High knees!" he calls, and I can hear the sound of everyone slapping their thighs as they lift them as close to their chests as they can. It's hard to breathe with a mouth guard, and it's hard to breathe in a helmet. Everything feels hot and trapped, and the only thing I want to do in the whole world right now is take off my shoulder pads and throw them down right there on the twenty-yard line because they're heavy and rubbing against Great-Grandpa Olson's dog tags and pushing down on me and making me feel even smaller than I already am.

Coach separates us into groups based on our positions, and I'm so glad I'm not Shane because he has to run full speed and smash into those blocking dummy pads that stand as tall and wide as an offensive center from the NFL. But he trots off like he can't wait to plow his shoulder in, even if it sends him bouncing off and flying two yards back, helmet thudding against the ground and bringing up grass.

We're running routes again. Coach is drawing quick lines on a whiteboard he holds in his hands. He swoops a line left then right and makes an X. "That's where you'll receive the ball," he says. I can hear my heart beating in my helmet.

"Sixth graders first," Coach says. "Marcus. Cyrus. Let's see if you've got what it takes to play A Team ball."

Marcus lines up and gives me a look like I better not mess this up. Assistant Coach Erikson snaps the ball, and I'm off, zigging right and swooping left just like Coach Matthews drew on his board. Then I'm looking back at Marcus. I see his eyes through the face mask, and they're locked right on me. Hard. I raise my sticky-gloved hand, and Marcus pulls back and snaps a throw, and I'm tracking its perfect spiral path through the air. I know this pass will hit my hands even if I don't try, and I don't want it to be Marcus's fault, and I don't want it to be the sticky gloves' fault either, so I find a place to stub my scrunched-up toe and tumble down, the ball flying over my head and bouncing head over tail.

"What the—? Cyrus! Oh my— Are you kidding me?" Marcus is yelling. "That was—"

"A perfect pass," I call back. "Another perfect pass! I just suck."

Marcus spits through his face mask. "You can say that again."

"Nonsense," Coach Matthews calls. "Get up. Run it again."

He makes us run it four more times, and I complete

one of the catches because I don't want to be too obvious.

"Beauty!" Coach Matthews calls. "That was a real beauty!" Then he tells us to take a rest and lines up a couple seventh graders to run the same route.

"What the heck, Cy?" Marcus says, spitting out his mouth guard.

I just shrug and say sorry and watch the seventh grade wide receiver complete the pass on the first try.

At the end of practice, Coach Matthews says he'll call us tomorrow to tell us if we're on the A or B Team. Then we have to line back up for touch-and-goes again, and my legs already burn from being sore on sore, and I don't want to breathe one more breath into this helmet. And it makes me wonder again about Parker, if he's in a cage and feels shut in and too hot and just wants to get out. I wish Dad would give in and take me to the humane society so I could see for myself and let Parker rest on my shoulder for just one second more.

I finish toward the end of the pack. Marcus and Shane finish at the front with the eighth graders, and they give each other a chest slam and *huh huh graaa* and walk off together without even saying goodbye, and I walk on wobbly legs to meet my dad in the parking lot and slump into the passenger seat.

"Sore?" he asks.

"Dead," I tell him. He laughs and starts the car, and

I loosen my cleats and angle the air-conditioning vent toward my sweaty, eye black–smudged face.

As we pull out, the coaches wave, and my dad honks the horn—two quick beeps. I see Marcus shake his head, and if I had a birthday wish left over, I might use it to wish I don't make the A Team, even if my name is Olson.

CHAPTER 6

New Guy

Before we go home, Dad says we're going to stop at the firehouse to meet the new guy. "We're getting pizza for lunch."

"OK," I say, but really I just want to go home. I'm tired, and I don't feel like saying goodbye to Mike and hello to someone new, because out of all the guys at the firehouse Mike is my favorite. He's been there from the beginning, and he doesn't care if I take the stairs or the ladder or if I ever do sit-ups on the gym mat.

We pull in just as Leo is stepping out of his green truck. "How'd it go this morning?" he asks. I nod and say it was OK and there are a lot of kids who are really good, so I'm not sure.

"But none of them are Olsons," he says and reaches out for a bump.

Then he claps my dad on the back the way Marcus does to Shane after a big block and says, "This new guy has big shoes to fill. Know anything about him?"

Dad shakes his head and tells Leo that the chief did the interview. I like Chief Reynolds, but he's only at the firehouse sometimes because he's busy doing what my dad calls office stuff. "I just know his name is Sam and he comes from Detroit," Dad says, and puts his arm around my shoulders.

We all walk to the door, and before I can start thinking what I always think when I walk through the front door of the firehouse, about how I was wrapped and crying and left here eleven years ago, I step in and see Mike and he's pointing to a piece of paper where the new guy is signing.

Except she's not a guy.

She has long wavy brown hair, and she's wearing a white V-neck T-shirt and jeans that stop at her ankle and yellow shoes that lift her an inch off the ground, but she still only reaches Mike's shoulder, and he's not even the tallest guy in the firehouse.

The door slams behind us and she spins around and reaches out her hand and says, "Hi, I'm Sam."

Leo squints his eyes. "Where's the new guy?"

"You're looking at her," Sam says.

"Firewoman?" Leo scoffs.

"Fire*fighter*," Sam says, but the way she says it makes it sound like she's actually saying *duh*.

My dad shakes her hand and says, "Chief Reynolds didn't tell us— I'm—I'm Brooks. Brooks Olson."

I can tell Leo still can't get over it. He kind of shakes his head and says to himself. "A firewoman? I've never heard of such a thing."

"Firefighter," she says again. "And you should get out more." That gets Mike and Roger and my dad laughing out loud now and clapping Leo on the back.

"That's the truth," Roger says.

But Leo's all serious and not laughing as he heads to meet the pizza delivery guy at the door, and I hear him mumble, "What can a firewoman do?"

Sam shakes her head and looks at me and says, "I'm going to hope he's not as dumb as he seems." Then she just kind of rolls her eyes and laughs him off and asks me what my name is.

I reach out my hand like Dad did and say, "I'm Cyrus. Cyrus Olson." She smiles and says hello and that it's nice to meet me.

"Football player?" she asks, and I reach up to the eye black on my cheeks.

"Yeah," I tell her.

Dad gives my hair a ruffle and says, "He just finished his middle school tryouts."

"Fun!" Sam says. But I'm thinking not.

Then she looks back at Dad and says, "I'm ready to get started. Where's my uniform?"

"Folded on the bench upstairs. When Cy moves his stuff over to locker two, you'll be locker five."

Dad gestures toward the staircase, but Sam walks over to the pole, looks back at us, says thanks and that she'll be down in a minute. Then she hops up and climbs arm over arm, her biceps bulging with each pull, until we hear her heels hit the floor above.

No one can believe it. No one can even say anything.

Then she squats and looks down through the hole at us. Her hair spills over her shoulders, and her voice comes soaring down the pole. "That's one thing a fire-*woman* can do." Dad gives a nod and says something about how the chief knows how to hire, but I don't even really hear it all because I'm still wondering how she made climbing up to the lockers look that easy.

Then I start thinking about how the whole locker numbers thing is kind of silly. Really I don't care about moving lockers at all, and I think Leo only does because he won't be last anymore. He'll go from five to four, and Sam will be last.

"I don't need to move all my stuff," I tell my dad. "Sam can just have Mike's old locker."

Before my dad can say anything, Leo blurts, "You don't want locker two?" He has three pizzas in his arms, and he's on his way to the kitchen.

I shake my head no because I don't actually want to be any closer to locker one. I already know I can't fill my dad's shoes, so I'm not about to try filling his locker.

"I'll take it," Leo says. "We can't give Mike's old locker to someone new." The way he says *new* gives me that not-right feeling down in my gut. But before I can say that lockers don't really matter, and that if Sam just takes locker two, then no one has to move at all, Leo's climbing arm over arm up the pole and I can hear the metal locker doors clanging upstairs.

I hear Leo tell her, "Locker five."

"Got it," she responds.

My dad and I must be thinking the same thing, and it's that we should probably be up there in case Leo says something that sounds kind of *Duh* again, because we both head for the stairs fast.

When we get to the top, Sam has her uniform draped over her arm and she's going toward the bathroom. We're all just kind of watching because there's a sign next to the door that has the figure of a man on it.

And that's it—we only have one bathroom at the firehouse. And even if we had more, we never would have needed to get one of those signs that has the figure in the dress.

She stops at the door and looks back at us. It's not a look that asks *Is it OK if I go in?* It's a look that says *I'm going in.* And she does. Then I hear her call out, "That sign just looks like a person to me!" She's right, and it makes me laugh because now the sign seems kind of silly.

Leo snorts, but my dad goes over and rips the sign right off the wall. It was only held with Velcro tape, but it rips off loud, like it's making a point.

"Guess we can get rid of this."

Leo snorts again and slams locker number two. I want to tell him it's just a locker and it's just a bathroom.

Dad and I hustle back down the stairs, and Leo slides, landing on his feet. We hear the bathroom door close, and when Sam slides down and lands on her feet, her hair is pulled back in a ponytail and the suspenders that I'm used to seeing over the guys' shoulders are up over her new firefighter T-shirt.

Leo huffs a little laugh, but Sam catches him and looks him right in the eyes.

"Listen," she says. "I know you think a woman in

this uniform doesn't look right." She snaps her suspenders. "But I assure you I can fight fires. Been doing it a long time in firehouses bigger than this one. And I sure as heck can fight small thoughts like the ones you're thinking right now."

"I . . . I didn't say . . ."

I've never heard Leo stutter before, and I have to concentrate to not laugh at him. But then I hear my dad let loose a short, deep chuckle, so I do too.

"What? What?" Leo says.

My dad starts passing out paper plates and opening the boxes of pizzas and he just raises his eyebrows at Leo and I know what he's thinking. He's thinking that even though Leo can do more push-ups than anyone and can do touch-and-goes back and forth forever with his leg muscles bulging out from his gym shorts, his uniform has never actually seen a major fire. Not more than a two-alarm, not yet. So who knows if he's brave like that. Brave like use-your-huge-muscles-when-it-really-counts kind of brave.

The pizza is good, and I eat two slices before everyone else finishes one. Leo says he's not really hungry and leaves half his piece on the plate. He tells us he's going to pump some iron and climbs back up the pole. I can hear him huffing through sit-ups and chin-ups and all the other kind of ups he does.

Dad puts another piece on Sam's plate and grabs one for himself.

"So, what position do you play?" she asks me.

"Wide receiver."

"Just like his old man," Dad adds.

She takes a bite. "That's great," she says. "As long as you love it."

My cheeks turn hot, and I wonder if she's like Grandma, who can see all the secrets deep inside me, but she's just chewing her pizza and drinking water from one of the firehouse mugs.

"My sisters and I all ended up being exactly what we said we wanted to be when we were five," Sam says. "It's just what we kept loving."

"You always wanted to be a firefighter?" I ask. And I can feel my heartbeat pick up the pace because I'm eleven already and I don't know what I want to be when I grow up. I know it's a not a firefighter. Or a wide receiver. Or anything where you have to read too much.

"Yup," she says. "Can't say my parents were too excited about the idea, but I know a thing or two about not doing what's expected of me, about branching out on my own."

I'm looking at her, hoping she'll keep talking because I like her story and the way she's telling it. "Like what?" I ask.

"Like when I was supposed to be taking dance classes with my big sister, I would sneak across the street to the firehouse and peek in the side windows at the red trucks. I loved the ladders and the long hoses. I loved the siren sound."

My dad nods his head like they're part of some club that just gets it. And I don't. Trucks and ladders and sirens make me feel sweaty and nervous, but the way Dad and Sam are sitting, cross-legged with their suspenders and firefighter T-shirts, telling stories of blasting hoses before fires spread and pumping foam to douse the flames, makes me positive that this is right where they belong.

Sam tips her head back for the last sip of water, and before she walks out of the kitchen I ask what her sisters grew up to be because I need all the ideas I can get.

"Ballerina and veterinarian."

My dad chuckles, but it's friendly. "You're kidding me. A firefighter, a ballerina, and a veterinarian?"

"I know," and she laughs a little with him. "It's like we all got to stay five years old."

Those jobs don't give me any ideas about what I want to be when I grow up, because the thought of dancing in public makes me feel like fainting, and even though I love Parker and wish my dad would loosen up on his no-pets-no-way policy, I don't love needles or blood or waiting rooms. But she gives me another kind of idea, an idea like sneaking out of dance class and branching out on your own.

An idea about doing something I'm not supposed to do, but I decide, right in that minute, that I'm doing it anyway.

CHAPTER 7

The 7

At the firehouse the next day, Leo asks me if I've heard from the coach yet. I tell him no and he says, "How were the other wide receivers? Were you keeping up?"

I shrug and look down at the black Vans I got last summer. The right one is scuffed up from the very day I got them, the day Marcus tried to teach me how to skateboard and I dragged my toe down his driveway to keep from getting going too fast.

Roger's got a football he's passing back and forth between his hands. "Want to toss it around the parking lot for a minute?"

"That's OK," I say. And I know this is my big moment, because if I'm a star at anything, I'm a star at faking. So I look up and say, "I think Marcus and Shane are running routes at Marcus's house today while we wait to hear about the teams."

"You want to go?" Dad asks. He's raising his eyebrows because I haven't asked to run routes in their backyards since they started running full speed and bouncing off each other's chests and smacking their helmets together just for fun.

"Guess maybe I should."

Dad tussles my hair and says, "Atta boy."

"Meet you at home for dinner," I tell him.

Even though I've never straight-out lied to Dad and I'm starting to get that uneasy feeling in my stomach, I keep walking toward the door, right over the spot where I was left eleven years ago, the spot where we found Parker trembling with his tail between his legs, and I continue on down the street.

I look back to make sure no one is watching, then turn right toward the humane society instead of left toward Marcus's backyard and walk fast with my eyes down.

I'm remembering every little detail I can about Parker—his brown-and-white patched fur, short and rough like wires, his whimpering, and his ribs—and before I know it, I'm running, and I tell myself that this counts as running a route, and it's the only route that makes me feel like it's right where I belong.

* * *

The humane society is clean like a doctor's office, with tile floors and hard plastic chairs and a front desk with a lady wearing a green smock and a big smile. Dogs are barking in the back, and I listen hard through all the yips and howls for Parker's whimper. And now that I'm this close, I feel like I can't wait one more minute to see him and tell him I came back and everything is going to be OK because *humane* means *nice* and they'll find him a good family.

The lady at the desk tells me her name is Max, and that makes me think of Sam and how you just shouldn't ever assume anything. Max asks how she can help, and I tell her I'm here to visit Parker and I describe his brown fur and white-dipped tail.

"And who are you?" She smiles wide again, and it reminds me of when we visited my grandma in the hospital after her stroke. The nurse made Dad show his driver's license, then checked to make sure we were on the family list. We signed our names on a clipboard, and she gave us sticky name tags with Grandma's room number printed on them. I remember looking at the list as the nurse peered over the glasses on her nose and feeling relieved that even if I didn't look like any other Olson, Cyrus was on the list, that I was family, because Grandma and my dad said so.

And I'm wondering if I'll have to show Max some proof that I belong to Parker.

I smile and say I'm Cyrus.

"Are you here for the volunteer walking?" she asks.

I nod my head because a walk with Parker sounds perfect. I'm trying to look past her and past the front desk and down the hall to where I hear the barking while she writes *Cyrus* on a name tag, peels it off, and sticks it right over my heart.

"Welcome," she says. "You can wait with the other volunteers until we're ready to bring the dogs out for their walks."

She points to the plastic chairs, and I count seven girls that I didn't even notice when I walked in. They're huddled around, talking, and they're all taller than four feet eight inches.

I'm not great at adding myself to circles, so I just kind of stand off to the side, with one ear listening to their conversation and another still listening for Parker down the hall.

One of the girls is wearing bright orange Crocs and talking about a book she's reading, and it makes me take one step back, because even if I were good at adding myself into circles, I'm definitely not good at talking about books.

Another girl, in a pink dress with wavy brown hair

and bright eyes, looks up and says hi, and it takes me a second to realize she's saying hi to me.

The girl next to her has short hair cut above her ears and green pants with suspenders, and she's waving me over. I can feel my face getting hot because the only girls I ever really talk to are my grandma and Milly, and I don't think they count.

I walk over slowly, hoping the dogs come running and barking down the hall dragging their leashes, ready for their walks, because I can't think of one single thing to say.

"Hey, Cyrus!" The girl who knows my name is tall and strong and wearing a swim team T-shirt with Joseph Lee Heywood's face printed on the front. I have no idea who she is, and the fact that she knows my name is making me feel even more awkward and weird. Then she points to my chest. "Your name tag."

I look down at *Cyrus* and say, "Oh, duh."

And all seven of them crack up, but they aren't cracking up in a way that makes my cheeks burn hotter, they're cracking up in a way that makes me crack up too, and all of a sudden I'm in their circle and even though they're still talking about that book, I don't feel like stepping back behind the edges.

I read all their name tags. Orange Crocs is Lou, a family nickname that just stuck, she tells me. Pink dress is Ruth. Green pants is Elli. Swim team is Katherine. There's June, who asks to borrow Lou's book for her book club, and DeeDee, who has dark curls and a full tote bag with sunscreen sticking out, and Alexis, with a smile so wide it seems to take up her entire face.

"This is your first time here," Alexis says, and it's not a question.

"We've been doing this together since sixth grade," DeeDee adds. "No one else ever really shows up, but we're here every Tuesday and Friday."

I decide not to tell them that I don't even start sixth grade for another four days.

"Yeah," I say. "First time."

"We're the HS 7." June pushes the glasses up her nose and smiles and reaches out her hand to shake mine, and I reach out too.

"Humane Society 7," DeeDee explains. "But we just go by *The 7*."

"Welcome." Elli nods, and then they're all saying *welcome*, even if it's just with their eyes and smiles.

Then I hear the claws on the floor and hard, slobbery panting as Max from the front desk, and a man in a green smock, each with six dogs pulling on leashes, come barreling down the hall.

And before I know it, Parker's nose is right there on my shoulder, and he's wagging his tail so fast his whole body is going, and then he pees on the tile floor and it pools around my Vans and I don't even care because he remembers me.

The man runs to get rags and a spray bottle of cleaner, but DeeDee is faster and pulls a wad of paper towels from her bag to wipe up the mess.

"It looks like he knows you," she says.

Parker pants hot breath down my neck. "He does."

The 7 take the leashes, but they let me take Parker, and we head for the back door across the parking lot to the trails that wind through the woods behind the Carleton College playing fields.

Parker jumps and wags his tail. I can still count his ribs, but he doesn't feel as skinny as he was when he showed up at the firehouse. He still shrinks away and pulls his tail between his legs when a bird surprises him and flaps its wings loudly out of a tree, or one of The 7's shoes gets too close to his paws, but he doesn't whimper and hang his head like before.

The girls talk about what teachers they'll have, and back-to-school shopping and Labor Day sales, and favorite ice cream flavors as we walk. I learn that they're all going into eighth grade at Joseph Lee Heywood Middle School.

"How about you?" Alexis asks.

I tell them I'm starting sixth grade, and they don't laugh or smirk or try to walk fast and lose me in the dust or anything, they just ask what teachers I have, and I tell them the names I can remember.

My English teacher, Mr. Hewett, is the best, they tell me.

I decide not to tell them that it's too late for me and English class. I'm four days away from sixth grade, and I still can't really read. Not the way other people can. Not like read-a-book-talk-about-it-and-share-it-with-your-friend-for-her-book-club kind of reading.

"Mr. Hewett's first assignment is going to be a review of the best book you've ever read," June tells me. "Just so you know. He does it every year."

"Almost every other teacher's first assignment is an essay on Joseph Lee Heywood," DeeDee says and rolls her eyes. "I'm using the one I wrote last year if we have to do that again, because seriously, if they can't come up with something new, neither can I."

"That school's obsessed with Joseph Lee Heywood," Alexis says. "If you ever get in trouble, just say, 'Joseph Lee Heywood was so brave,' and they'll forget that they were about to call your parents to complain about you being late to class."

That gets us all laughing again.

We walk around a bend in the trail, and Elli breathes

in deep. "Ahhhhh. Fresh air and—"

"Cheerios!" they all shout.

"Forget Joseph Lee Heywood," Katherine says. "*That* is the best thing about Northfield." She takes in another big breath.

And she's right. It is the best. Every afternoon at exactly three forty-five, the whole town starts to smell like Cheerios being pumped into the air from the big smokestack at the Malt-O-Meal factory that towers high above our little town, and everyone stops whatever they're doing and takes a big whiff of it before they continue on. I don't know any other towns that have their own flavors.

Parker pulls on the leash and sniffs around a bush on the side of the trail. I scratch behind his ears, and the girls go back to talking about an end-of-summer sleepover they're planning, and I'm wondering what my favorite book could be and how I can fake a good review for Mr. Hewett.

The 7 laugh and laugh and laugh. And I'm thinking that this might be my first time at the humane society, but I'm definitely coming back, even if it means faking around my dad every Tuesday and Friday because walking next to Parker is right where I belong.

When we bring the dogs back, Max meets us at the door, and I bend down and look right in Parker's big brown eyes. And I tell him I'll be back. I promise.

He parks his nose right on my shoulder, and I wrap my arms around his neck.

And that's when I hear the sirens.

CHAPTER 8

Smoke

I've never been in trouble before because I figure I was enough trouble as a seven-pound, four-ounce baby, so I should probably give my dad a break now. Plus, my stomach always has this way of flipping and flopping and telling me when what I'm doing is wrong.

Marcus and Shane haven't been in much trouble either, but it's because they're sneaky, not because they're angels.

One time they decided to steal a candy bar from the grocery store, and once they wrote on the bathroom stall in permanent marker. Both times I was pretty good at walking the other way and pretending I didn't know them or what was going on. It left that feeling in my

stomach, though, to know that they were doing something bad and even though I wasn't a part of it, I kind
of was.

But I'm the one in trouble now.

I'm sitting on the kitchen stool and Dad is standing
with his arms folded, looking down at me. He's not yelling, he's not even talking, but I can tell he's thinking
and thinking and thinking of what a terrible thing I did
because he's shaking his head.

"You weren't where you said you'd be."

I'm looking down at my shoes.

"I always need to know where you are, Cy."

I nod my head, but my eyes are still on my Vans,
studying the old scuff marks on the right toe and thinking that I didn't even want to try skateboarding, but
Marcus made the call and Shane defended him and
before I knew it I was flying down the driveway and
dragging my toe and scuffing up my new shoes.

He takes a big breath and I'm pretty sure he's going
to ask me a hundred questions, and even though I can't
imagine my dad getting loud, I bet his voice will rise
with each one until he's yelling at me.

But instead he starts telling me, in his regular, calm
voice, what happened at the firehouse.

"It was a half hour until the end of my shift," he says.

His voice is still steady and normal, but I can't look at him. I stare at my hands and then out the window and right before I glance back down at my shoes I hear a *ding* and my Dad's cell phone vibrates on the counter. It's probably a voice mail from Coach Matthews, so I cross my fingers and shove them under my legs on the stool and say *B Team, B Team* in my head.

"I was thinking we'd go get your school supplies tonight," Dad says. "That's when the call came in. We sounded the siren and hopped in the engine. We were headed toward Eleven Chestnut Street, sirens blaring."

Then he pauses for a long time. Or at least it seems really long. And I'm starting to feel really bad that he was thinking about buying me school supplies tonight while I was off faking him out.

"I called Marcus's mom to tell you to go to Grandma's after running routes. She said that Marcus and Shane were playing in the yard, but you hadn't been there all day."

I hang my head lower, mostly because I hate that I made my dad worried, but a little bit because I'm nervous about the message on Dad's phone.

"So when we pulled into Eleven Chestnut Street and saw the smoke, I was still thinking about where you were," he continues.

I nod.

"We flung open the doors and unwound the hose. The family was already out in the yard, and asking us questions. And I was worrying about what could have happened to you on the way to Marcus's house."

Dad tells me to look at him. His eyes are watery, and I don't know if it's because of the smoke or because he's sad.

"The fire was small and easy to extinguish, which was lucky," he says.

I've never been in trouble before, but I'm positive it would be better if he would just yell at me and tell me I was grounded.

Imagining Dad worrying about me is way worse.

"Where were you?"

I look at his watery eyes, and I can't believe how easily one lie turns into two, because I know if I tell him about Parker and the humane society he'll tell me again about not getting attached, and how he said no, and then that's it. I'll never get to walk Parker again. And I promised him I'd be back.

"I—I found out at tryouts that I'm going to have to write a review of the best book I've ever read in Mr. Hewett's English class. I thought I might want to read something new." I glance up quick at his face to see if he's buying it.

He shifts his weight and raises his eyebrows.

"I was at the library. But I didn't find anything."

He lets out a little snort and pulls me into a hug that lifts me right off the stool. He doesn't give hugs like this that much, and it feels good and bad because now there are two lies edging their way between us.

"Don't ever do that to me again," he says low, right next to my ear. "My old heart can't take it."

Then he lets me go and turns around to look at his cell phone. "Well, well," he says. And I almost fake that I have to go to the bathroom so I don't have to stand next to Dad when Coach Matthews tells me what team I'm on because no matter what, it's going to stink. If I make the B Team, I'll have fewer practices and fewer hits and fewer people on the sidelines watching me fumble, but then there will be an Olson on the B Team, and it'll be my fault. If Coach Matthews gives me a spot on the A Team, I'll have to practice three days a week and everyone on the team will know I'm only there because of my dad, and Marcus will roll his eyes and spit every time I drop the ball, but maybe my dad will be proud.

Dad pushes speaker and sets the phone between us. "Brooks. Cyrus. This is Coach Matthews."

I'm holding my breath. But then he says it. B Team. I'm on the B Team. I just didn't quite make the cut. I need a year to get stronger and more confident, and he hopes I come back out for the A Team next year. Practices are Tuesday and Friday, starting this Tuesday, after the first day of school. And I wince because Tuesday and Friday are volunteer walk days at the humane society with The 7. With Parker.

"I'm sorry, Brooks," Coach says. Then the voice mail is over.

I look up at my dad. "I'm sorry too," I say.

He looks right in my eyes, and I'm blinking fast because I think I feel tears starting to burn and I don't want them leaking out. "Coach Matthews shouldn't be sorry. You shouldn't be sorry. I don't know why everyone is saying they're sorry." He clears his throat. "You did your best, Cy. I'm proud of you."

That makes me feel even worse, so I nod fast and say OK and do the jiggly have-to-pee dance and disappear down the hall.

That night, Dad walks by my bedroom door and peeks in.

"Hey, Cy, haven't you read dozens of books? Can't you just choose one of those to write about?"

And it's amazing how two lies can turn into three,

because I say yes, even though I haven't read any books ever—not really, anyway.

"If you want to read something new, didn't Grandma just give you a book for your birthday?" he asks.

"Oh yeah."

Wonder is on my dresser, and it's thicker than the two padded wide receiver gloves stacked next to it.

"Just read that one," he says.

"OK."

I roll over, and now my eyes are getting all watery again because that feels like a bigger lie than Parker and the library. It feels deeper down and impossible to pull up and show him—that I can't. I can't just read that one.

I hear his footsteps down the hall, but I don't want him to walk away yet. I want him to come back and keep talking to me. I don't even care about what.

"Hey, Dad?"

His footsteps return and stop outside my door. "I'm here."

"Whatever happened at Eleven Chestnut Street?"

He sighs. "Young kid playing with matches. Burned it down too close to his finger. Got scared and threw it in the trash."

I shake my head because I know what happens next. Fire spreads quick. It catches. You have to act fast.

And my dad *is* fast. Even when his head is full of worrying about where I am and if I'm OK. He stopped that fire before it spread because he's brave like that. Brave like stand-close-enough-to-burn-you brave.

CHAPTER 9

Eating Lefty

Tonight is a Grandma–Cy sleepover night, the last one before school starts, and even though I tell her to wait for me so I can help, she has the couch pulled out into a bed before I get there. I don't know how she takes off all the cushions and pulls the mattress out with her left hand, or how she drags her right foot around the whole bed, tucking in the sheet. But every sleepover it's ready for me.

"Na na na!" she says when I walk in. She's sitting in her chair, but she pulls her left hand back behind her head like she's throwing a football.

"It's just the B Team, Grandma."

She looks right at me and says, "Na na na na." And I know what she's saying. She's saying *B isn't so bad.* I don't explain to her that there is no C Team and that no one gets cut from the B Team. But something tells me that even if she knew all that, she'd still be proud of me.

"Thanks, Grandma," I say.

I reach down to hug her and she says, "Na na na na," again. Sometimes I have to make a hundred guesses, but today I know exactly what she's saying. *Tell me what's wrong.*

"Nothing," I mumble and shake my head. But she's waiting for a better answer. She pretends to throw a football again and raises her eyebrows like *Tell me more.*

"It's going to be awesome." I try a smile but it feels fake on my face.

She scrunches up her forehead. She doesn't believe me.

"I'm not as good as Dad."

She leans in and whispers, "Na na na na na na."

And I think she's saying exactly what Sam said. *As long as you love it.*

Then she points to her records and I go run my finger along the spines, and in my head I spell out *P-A-R-K-E-R*, then pull out the record I land on. Nina Simone, *Wild Is the Wind.* Grandma puts her left hand to her heart and closes her eyes. The last time I pulled a Nina Simone record from the shelf was before Grandma's stroke. That was the day she told me about how her parents gave her classical piano lessons, but really her heart loved jazz and she wanted to be just like Nina Simone and play at Carnegie Hall. When I raised my eyebrows at her to ask if she ever did, she shook her head and said, "My heart also loved raising your dad."

I drop the needle on the record, and Grandma's left hand starts playing along in the air with Nina Simone.

Milly knocks and comes in with two steaming plates from the dining room. "Dinner for two!" she announces.

Sometimes we eat in the dining room with my grandma's friends and they all pinch my cheeks even though I'm eleven years old and say how handsome I am and give me their extra scoops of ice cream. And sometimes we eat, just us, in my grandma's apartment and watch the Vikings or the Twins on TV with the sound off and a record playing.

Grandma's eating with her left hand, and I try to eat lefty too. It feels wrong and frustrating, like pinchy cleats or too-big shoulder pads, but I'm thinking that if I could erase my Grandma's stroke, then I'd run every route, catch every pass, and eat lefty every day.

I flick through the channels and Grandma yells, "Na!" at the Twins game. We're playing the Oakland A's and we're up three to one in the third inning, and my grandma whoops and cheers as if it's already the playoffs and as if the Twins even have a chance.

The count is three and two, and when the umpire stoops down in his position, my grandma pushes up slowly from her chair and limps a step closer to the TV and watches like she's going to make sure he's making the right calls.

"Na na na!" she exclaims, and wags her finger at ball four.

"Grandma," I say. "It's only the third inning."

That gets her laughing so hard that tears squeeze from the corners of her eyes, and we laugh so long that we miss the next out and all the commercials and somehow the Twins are up at bat again and Nina Simone is singing about breaking down and letting it all out.

After the game, I show Grandma my sixth-grade schedule. She runs her finger over *Mr. Hewett, English*. And *Ms. Martin, Math*. "Na na?" she says. "Na!" and points to the record player. Music.

"We don't have music every quarter, Grandma," I tell her. "I think we rotate with art, gym, and health."

She rests her head back against her chair and says, "Na na." And I know my grandma, and I know what she's saying. She's saying *Damn it*.

It's getting dark, and I'm getting tired, but before I turn out the lights, Grandma opens and closes the palm of her left hand like a book. She's asking me about *Wonder*, but I pretend I can't figure out what she's saying, and I feel awful about it because she gets upset when she can't communicate.

"Na na!" She opens and closes her hand again and brings it close to her face, and I just can't pretend anymore.

"Oh, my book? I'm going to start it soon, Grandma."

She raises her eyebrows and looks deep down in me. But she just pats my shoulder and turns off the light, and I think I know what we both might be wishing— 'that she could read it out loud to me, chapter by chapter, into the night like she used to. Because with her reading to me like that, with her voice that rose and fell and changed for every character, I could follow the story, and my stomach didn't get so uneasy when the teacher would ask me questions the next day.

Grandma squeezes my hand to say good night, and I tell her I can help her to the bedroom, but she says a sharp "Na!" that means *Don't you dare.* So I drag up the covers on the pullout couch, and I'm thinking about school starting and whether Mr. Hewett will make us read something in class the first day and what Marcus and Shane will say when they see me because they haven't called since I didn't make the cut.

And before I know it, I'm making up a new plan, a new fake, to get out of B Team practice. To see Parker.

CHAPTER 10

First Day

This is the first year my dad says it's OK to walk to school by myself in the morning and back home after practice. Our house, my grandma's apartment, and the firehouse are all less than five minutes away, so it's impossible to get lost. It feels good walking down the street on my own, but I have big butterflies in my stomach because school is hard, especially those first few days, when I meet my new teachers and I have to figure out how to get through one more year of faking it. The butterflies are flapping extra fast today, though, because I've got a fake planned to get out of practice this afternoon. And if it doesn't work, my dad will find out, and I'll never see Parker again.

I know my dad is watching me from the front

window as I walk toward school. I can feel it. He might look like a tall, tough-guy football player, but not everyone is exactly how they look on the outside. Inside he's the guy who held me at the hospital one last time, and took me home to keep forever. Before I turn the corner, I stop and look back and give him a little wave. He ducks down quick and tries to hide, but he knows I caught him watching.

I wait until he slowly stands back up and gives me a little closed-lipped smile through the window and raises his big hand to say goodbye. Then I turn the corner.

Lots of kids are walking toward Joseph Lee Heywood Middle School, and long yellow buses pull into the circle out front.

I pass by the tall flagpole, and it reminds me of my great-grandpa Olson fighting a war against the Nazis, and I can feel his dog tags resting on my chest beneath my shirt. They're supposed to be making me feel brave.

Instead, I'm feeling kind of hot and wishing I hadn't worn jeans and wondering if I have time to run home and change into shorts because it still feels like summer and everyone else is wearing shorts, but I'm afraid I'd miss the first the bell and I guess I'd rather be hot than late. So I walk through the open front doors.

Even though I've known almost everyone in my

sixth-grade class since pre-K, I'm feeling a little sweaty and uncomfortable and heart-poundy like I do when I'm under my football pads. My hands are all fumbly too, which isn't good because it's hard enough to understand this schedule without my hands shaking the paper all over the place.

I have homeroom in 102 with Mr. Hewett, who is also my English teacher. Even though I already know where that is, the halls aren't quiet and empty now like they were when I faked a bathroom trip during tryouts, and that new clean smell is already gone. Now it's crowded with lots of kids who are all taller than four feet eight inches and shouting one another's names and, "You cut your hair!" and "You got your braces off!" And instead of smelling like the cleaner we use to scrub the firehouse floor, it smells like the puffs of cologne that salespeople spray when you walk through the department stores in the Mall of America. And I'm wondering if you're supposed to start wearing cologne in middle school, and how do you figure something like that out?

I see a couple kids from last year, and they already seem to know where they're going. No one else is holding a schedule, and they're all fist-bumping and asking how summer was.

I see Marcus and Shane talking with some of the big

kids from tryouts. The A Team. I wave, but they don't see me, and between us is a crowd of seventh and eighth graders who are comparing arm tans and sipping out of to-go cups from the coffee shop on Division Street. I guess you start drinking coffee in middle school too.

Then I see three of the Humane Society 7 girls huddled and comparing schedules. They don't have their name tags on, but I remember them all.

Alexis catches my eye and says, "Hey! It's Cyrus! Parker's Cyrus!"

And that gives me that same good feeling I got when I caught Dad watching me through the window.

Ruth and Katherine wave and smile and tell me to have a good first day.

"See you later?" Ruth asks. And I nod because today is Tuesday. A humane society volunteer walk day, and I've got my plan to get there.

I turn around too fast to see if Marcus and Shane are still there, and I go face-first into some tall kid's book bag.

"Sorry," I say.

He looks down and shakes his head. "Watch where you're going."

"What's your name?" one of his friends asks.

"Cyrus. Olson. Cyrus Olson," I say. I happen to be standing right beneath my dad's picture in the trophy case.

"Like, Olson Olson?" he says and points to my dad. I nod.

The book bag guy laughs. "Don't think he has his dad's coordination."

The whole group of them starts laughing but not the kind of laughter that The 7 laughs, the kind that pulls you into the circle. It's the kind that pushes you out, and I can't think of one single thing to say, so I just keep walking toward Mr. Hewett's room.

Before I get there, I see a boy crouched under the water fountain. He has his book bag turned around the wrong way so it rests on his front, and his knees are tucked up to his chin. He's studying a wrinkled schedule. His lips move when he reads, and his finger points to the schedule, then taps the side of his head. He doesn't seem aware that other kids are staring at him and trying to hide their laughs.

"Who's that?"

"What's he doing?"

Marcus and the guys from the A Team come over and circle around and say, "What's wrong with him?" One guy even points and laughs out loud, then pretends he has to use the water fountain, splashing drops of water down on the kid's schedule.

"Oh, sorry, didn't see you there," he says.

The kid doesn't even look up. He just keeps reading

and wrinkling his schedule and pulls his knees closer to his chest. His skin is dark, not a summer-tan kind of dark, but a that's-how-it-always-is kind of dark. He wears rectangular-rimmed glasses and Velcro shoes and has black hair that sticks up in spikes.

Marcus nudges me with his elbow and says, "Sorry about the cut." And it makes my stomach settle a little because even if we aren't on the same team and he's frustrated with my butterfingers, I think we're still the friends we've always been.

"The elementary school is on the other side of town." One of the guys snickers at the kid under the fountain, and when I look up to see who it is, I realize I'm in their little group—Marcus, Shane, a bunch of guys from the A Team, and me, and we're all looking down at the boy. And this circle doesn't feel like The 7 either. It feels tight and hard to wiggle out of, like pinchy cleats.

The bell rings, and everyone starts moving again. Teachers stand outside their classroom doors and help kids read their schedules, pointing them in different directions.

Mr. Hewett is tall and skinny and bald, and wears little round glasses that make him look smart. He smiles at us and says, "Welcome," as we enter the room.

Marcus points to an empty table, and even though I don't like sitting in the way back because teachers always call on those kids first, I follow, and sit between him and Shane.

I know almost everyone in the class from last year. Addison and Hadleigh sit in the front. They have matching teal-blue streaks through their ponytails and are wearing soccer T-shirts. They've always been the best players in the grade, so I'm not surprised when they tell everyone they made the A Team.

Chris and Zander sit at the table next to us. Zander's hair is longer than it was last year, and Chris has sunglasses with orange reflective lenses sitting on top of his head. His parents own an outdoor shop up in the Boundary Waters, so Chris always has cool gear. For our end-of-year fifth-grade camping trip, they donated a headlamp to each tent group. Chris taught us how to adjust them to our heads and twist the light so it shines straight on, and how to tilt it down toward the ground. At first, I thought they were just the show-offy version of a trusty flashlight, the kind that we have at our house if the power goes out. But then, when it got dark and I had to go pee in the woods and fumble with the zipper on the tent, I realized they weren't just show-offy, they were actually pretty handy, especially if you're a little scared of the dark. The dead-of-night kind of dark.

Everyone is talking loud about summer camp and water parks and comparing new pocket folder designs.

Nora has a whole set of fine-tip Sharpie markers in every color of the rainbow, and she's writing her name on top of all her new notebooks. Joel and Benji are reaching over, each trying to snatch a color from her, because everyone knows labeling your new stuff in Sharpie is the best, but Nora swats away their hands.

Then Mr. Hewett comes in the classroom with the kid from under the water fountain. He points to an empty seat at a table in the middle of the room next to Patrick and Curtis. "You can sit right there for now," he whispers. The boy is still wearing his book bag on his front. He nods and says OK and walks around the tables and takes his seat.

Mr. Hewett welcomes us to Joseph Lee Heywood Middle School and tells us he's so excited for the year ahead, and I can tell he means it because he leans forward like he's ready to jump right in. Plus, he smiles a real smile that sends little ripples to the corners of his mouth.

He asks us to push all the tables back and stand in a big circle. It takes us forever, but when we're finally in a circle I end up between Marcus and Shane and directly across from the new kid. Mr. Hewett has a foam football with the Carleton College Knights logo, and he's holding it with his fingers between the laces like maybe he's thrown a few long passes before.

"Let's get to know each other," he says, which makes us laugh because except for him and the new kid we all know one another already.

When we get the ball, we're supposed to say our name and one thing about ourselves, then toss it, underhand, to someone else around the circle.

Marcus scoffs. "Underhand."

Mr. Hewett glances over, but Marcus looks off and whistles like he's innocent and points at me, like I was the one who said something out of turn on the first day.

I know Marcus is joking and some kids are snickering, but for some reason it makes me feel hot, and not just because I'm wearing jeans. Mr. Hewett gives a little disappointed-looking face to both of us and shakes his head, like we're going to be the ones to watch. I take a little half step away from Marcus, but that means I'm a half step closer to Shane, who is trying to stop laughing, but his shoulders are still shaking.

Mr. Hewett continues. "When you toss the ball, underhand, try to pick someone you don't know." Everyone kind of giggles again.

"OK, OK. I don't know *anyone*," he says, "so I'll start. I'm Mr. Hewett, and I love ice cream." Someone lets out a little snort. "No, I don't think you understand how much. I bet I love it more than all of you combined." We all say, "Nooooooo," and he responds, "Yessssssss," and I already like him and wish even more that Marcus hadn't made him look at me with that disappointed face.

He tosses the ball to Zander, who says his older brother is going to Carleton College right in town this fall, so he can go visit his dorm room anytime. Zander tosses it to Addison, who says she loves soccer. Addison tosses it to Nora, who says she went to art camp this summer and learned how to throw a pot. The whole class cracks up, including me, because I'm picturing her throwing pots across a kitchen. Nora kind of giggles too. "Throw a pot means make something out of clay on a spinning wheel," she explains. "Pottery."

Mr. Hewett nods and says, "Cool."

Everyone just keeps tossing the ball to someone they've known since pre-K, and no one is throwing to the boy from under the water fountain. And that makes my stomach feel all wrong and uncomfortable.

And it's not like the new boy is looking down at his Velcro shoes and avoiding a pass like I do on the field. He's following Mr. Hewett's foam football, and I can see that he's mouthing everyone's name after they say it, like he's trying to memorize the room.

Geordie likes video games, which is the same thing he says every year. Joel got a new mountain bike this summer. Hadleigh's favorite color is teal, and she tugs on her streaked ponytail as evidence.

Then she looks around the circle, shrugs her shoulders like *What the heck?* and tosses the ball to the new kid. He fumbles it a little. The ball bobbles back and forth between his hands a couple times, then it drops and bounces end over end around the circle until he leaps and pounces on it with all fours.

He's the first to laugh, but everyone else does too.

"My name is Eduardo." He chuckles. And I'm secretly hoping he tells us where he's from, where you get a name like Eduardo and learn how to say it the way he does, all rolls and soft stops that seem like they barely escape his lips.

"And I obviously don't play football." He laughs again, and so does the class. "I like music."

Then he looks right at me and lobs the football. It sort of goes in my direction but falls short. Marcus reaches out and catches it just before it hits the floor.

"I guess you really *don't* play football," Marcus says, but he doesn't say it in the fun way we've all been laughing along with. He says it like he's eight feet tall and the new kid is one foot tall and his voice has to reach all the way down and down and down to get to him. Like he's the king of the world and the new kid is dirt.

Shane and Marcus laugh. And we're squeezed in so tight to the circle, shoulder to shoulder, that their laughs bounce me a little, like I'm laughing too, but I'm not.

"I'm Marcus. I'm a quarterback. On the A Team."

The new kid giggles again and says, "It *would* take a football star to catch my wild pass."

Marcus snorts another little laugh. "Quarterbacks don't field passes. They do the passing. They create the plays. Everyone knows that."

The new kid shrugs his shoulders.

Then Marcus whispers under his breath, "Edweirdo," and hands the ball off to me.

I'm not sure if anyone else hears him, because the class is still kind of chuckling from the wild pass and Marcus saying, "Everyone knows that," but Shane does, and it makes him howl. He's laughing so hard that Mr. Hewett has to send him out of the circle to collect himself before rejoining us.

Shane struts out like he doesn't care one bit that the teacher had to speak to him on the first day of school, like he'd rather be in the hall than in some stupid class anyway. Like he's eight feet tall too. And I'm wondering what happened to Marcus and Shane when we stopped two-hand touch and started full tackle. Did they bash their heads together so hard that their brains rattled around in their helmets and it made them kind of mean? Or is it the A Team that got into their brains?

I wish Marcus had passed the ball to someone else because even though we've been friends since the day his cat was stuck up a tree, I don't want Mr. Hewett to know that. It feels bad being shoulder to shoulder with him right now.

Plus, all of a sudden, I can't think of anything to share about myself. Nothing.

I toss the ball back and forth between my hands, thinking, and my brain can't come up with one single thing.

"Your name?" says Mr. Hewett. A few kids chuckle, but they try to hide it because they don't want to be sent out with Shane.

"Cyrus."

Then Marcus nudges me and whispers, "You play football."

"I love dogs." It just kind of falls out of my mouth.

And Marcus shakes his head like I've just fumbled a perfect pass in the end zone.

At the end of the name game, Mr. Hewett asks if anyone can go around and say everyone's name and one thing about them. Every hand goes up because we all could have done that in the beginning, but Mr. Hewett calls on Eduardo.

All heads turn toward him because there's no way he could know all twenty-four of us when he's only just met us now.

He starts with Marcus and works his way around the

circle, looking each one of us in the eye. "You are Nora, and you throw pots. You are Chris, and you canoed ten miles this summer. You are Patrick, and you have three hamsters." He doesn't stop or stumble over any of us as he gets all the way back around the circle to me. "And you are Cyrus. You love dogs." The class gasps and claps and whispers, "How did he do that?"

He smiles and bows and pushes his glasses back up his nose, and Mr. Hewett is clapping wildly.

Everyone helps push the tables back together while Mr. Hewett chats quietly with Shane. Marcus nudges me and whispers, "And I'm Edweirdo, and I don't belong here." He snickers and I make myself give a little fake laugh and it makes me feel itchy and terrible all period.

The rest of the day goes OK even though switching rooms and teachers for every subject is confusing. Most of our classes are in the same hall, but we have to go upstairs for science and downstairs for lunch. Last period of the day is English, back in Mr. Hewett's room.

I sit at the same table with Marcus and Shane because that's where I sat this morning, and I'm expecting Mr. Hewett to have us share about something we read this summer, so I start practicing in my head what I've memorized in case he calls on me. *I'm reading the fourth Harry Potter, where Harry is . . . well, you all know the story. Don't give anything away for me!*

But instead of asking us to share about what we've read, or handing us a paragraph and telling us to read it independently, then write about what it means to us, or explaining that he expects us to read a book every day like his bulletin board says, he asks us all to push in our chairs and join him on the rug.

Some of us are kind of looking around at one another because we haven't been to a rug area with a teacher since third grade with Ms. Havrika.

"Come on," he says, and he pulls a short stool over to the corner of the room where there's a purple rug and a bunch of pillows.

He tells us to gather around, and one by one we push in our chairs and find a seat on the rug. We're all kind of shrugging our shoulders like *What the heck?* because we're not eight years old anymore and we thought that middle school would be hard books and long vocabulary words and impossible pop quizzes.

Eduardo is sitting right up front and I'm behind him, next to Marcus and Shane, who stick out their legs and take up way too much space and start muttering about how they're too big for sitting on the floor.

Then Mr. Hewett pulls out a picture book and we all start to giggle.

"What?" he says. "Can't a grown guy love a picture

book?" Then he leans right in again and whispers, "I'm going to tell you a secret. I love picture books more than I love ice cream."

He's smiling a big smile that makes his eyes crinkle and I can tell it's the truth. It's not a fake. He rubs the cover of the book and says, "You all think you're too big for picture books, but let me tell you something. You're not. No one is."

Marcus shakes his head. Shane sighs like he's bored.

Mr. Hewett doesn't say anything else. He just waits until we're all quiet, then reads the cover. *Calvin Can't Fly: The Story of a Bookworm Birdie.*

He reads each page to us, standing to make sure we all see the pictures, letting his voice rise up and fall back down and speed along and get slower at all the right parts, and some of the book is funny and he gets us all laughing. And at the end, when all the birdies realize that even though Calvin doesn't seem to fit with the flock, he is a crucial part of their team, we all say, "Awwwwww."

And maybe it's because I know how Calvin feels— to not belong, to not fit quite right—I feel a tiny burn behind my eyes. The same burn I felt when my dad sat me down on the edge of my bed and told me what a stroke was and what to expect when we visited my grandma in the hospital. My dad told me then that it was OK to cry, so I did, and now when I look up I see Mr. Hewett's eyes are telling me the same thing. That it's OK to feel what I'm feeling. But I don't look at him long because I don't want to cry in school, especially over a funny picture book about a bookworm birdie. So I look away and by accident I lock eyes with Eduardo and I wonder if maybe he's feeling the same thing.

At the end of the period, Mr. Hewett tells us about our first assignment, the one The 7 told me about. I already know I'm writing mine on *Wonder*. I found a good summary online that I'll revise into my own words, with quotes and everything, and I know from fifth grade that every review has to make a point, so I'm making the point that every middle school kid should read this book. I give it two thumbs up.

He asks Curtis to pass out an assignment sheet, and Shane sneers and whispers, "Homework already?"

The bell rings and as we're packing up Mr. Hewett says, "And don't go thinking you're going to reuse a book report from last year or just watch the movie version and go from that. I have an excellent fake detector."

It makes my heart skip, but I don't look up at him or hesitate while zipping my book bag because I don't want to give anything away, like I'm the kid to watch with that fake detector turned on full blast.

"Best book you've ever read. Ever. You have a week. Use the assignment sheet. Make it good."

After school I watch as the buses pull up in front of the building and all the lucky kids who didn't try out for sports teams hop up the three steps and find a seat.

I go to the locker room with the athletes from every team yelling and fist-bumping and filling up their water bottles, and I change into my heavy pads and pinchy cleats and trot out to the field with Marcus and Shane.

Coach Matthews welcomes us to the official start of the season and tells us we'll split into A and B squads in a minute. "It's a Heywood tradition to wear your jerseys to school the day after you receive them," he says. There's a big cardboard box at his feet with folded uniforms piled to the top. "You guys will be looking sharp tomorrow." He begins passing them out, and when he gets to me, he gives me jersey number eighty-eight, just like my dad, and I wonder if it's his exact same one because it isn't new and still smells a little like a locker room.

Before he moves on to hand Shane his jersey, I hold out the note. I wrote it with a black pen and squished all the words onto the back of a fire department safety brochure, and signed *Brooks Olson* in my best cursive. I spent all night practicing his signature from an old

University of Minnesota football card that's pressed in an album between two yellowing newspaper articles about his team's big wins.

"My dad says sorry about the note. He couldn't find any paper, and I was running late. Dentist appointment. I have to leave early."

He squints at the note, then he squints at me.

"If you can call him and get me out of it, I'd much rather be here, Coach."

He smiles and pats my pads and says, "Atta boy. But you better go." I nod and he says I'll be reporting to Assistant Coach Erikson on Friday with the rest of the B Team.

I hate that I'm such a good faker. But at least this fake gets me something that makes me happy. This fake gets me Parker.

CHAPTER 11

Attached

I stop on the sidewalk to stuff my uniform into my bag and change out of my cleats. Then I hurry toward the humane society, listening for sirens because today is a firehouse day for my dad and if I hear that *wheeeee-ooooo*, I'm stepping into the next store or hiding down a skinny alley between buildings until the sirens stop.

My eyes are on the pavement, and I'm walking fast because I don't want to see anyone who knows my dad. Adults talk all the time about everything, and it would be just my luck that someone says, *I saw Cyrus the other day at three o'clock headed toward the humane society carrying his cleats.* I already know the looks my dad would give me. The ones that say *I was worried* and *I told you.*

Because he did tell me. He told me no more faking. No more not being where I'm supposed to be. He told me no dogs, and he told me no visiting. No getting attached.

Five of The 7 are in the waiting area when I get there, and they're talking about the first-day essay assignment.

"It's got to be boring for them too, right?" DeeDee says. "What teacher wants to see the same essay fifty times every year?"

"I don't think they read them," June adds. "I heard one year someone wrote, 'If you are actually reading this, please tell me,' in the middle of their essay, and it just came back with 'A-plus' on the top."

"I believe it," DeeDee says.

I get my sticker name tag from Max, and June says, "Be glad you have Mr. Hewett, Cyrus."

I nod my head like I'm glad, except I'm not really, because an essay about Joseph Lee Heywood is way easier to write than a review of a book you haven't actually read, especially when your teacher has an excellent fake detector.

Katherine and Elli rush through the front door. It slams again, and just then two vet techs with green smocks open the back doors. We hear the nails scratching on the floor and see the dogs pulling on their leashes and wagging their tails, excited for their walk.

"It's like they know it's Tuesday and they've been waiting for us," Katherine says.

Parker runs straight for me and parks his head on my shoulder. I rub his back and his tail is wagging so fast it knocks me off-balance and we end up in a pig pile on the humane society floor, which is the only pig pile that feels like it's right where I belong.

"Where's Rocky?" Katherine asks.

One of the vet techs looks at her with sad eyes. "We found her a home. A good one. With two little kids."

Katherine smiles and nods, but she has sad eyes too.

"Rocky was her favorite," Ruth tells me in a quiet voice.

And it's right there on Katherine's face why my dad says not to get attached.

I wrap the end of Parker's leash around my wrist and hold on tight.

There's a new mutt puppy that wasn't here last time. She's chewing on her skinny pink leash and tripping over it with every step.

"This baby was dropped off Friday night," Max tells us. "Healthy, excited pup. Lots of yipping and barking. Ready for her first walk."

The puppy is down on her front paws wagging her tail and playing. She hops toward Katherine and starts nibbling on her shoelace, untying her sneaker with her little puppy teeth. Katherine laughs and scoops the puppy up in her arms.

"She doesn't have a name yet," one of the vet techs says.

Katherine smiles and I can see that look on my dad's face. That face that says *Don't name it. It's not your dog.*

We gather all the leashes and follow the fast paws out the door, and then we're walking along the same trails as last time. Parker sniffs the grass and lifts his leg and never goes one inch beyond me even when all the other dogs run ahead and pull on their leashes. He stays right by my side, step by step. I'm checking my watch every few minutes because I can't be late to the firehouse.

Katherine jogs off with the new puppy bouncing along beside her. The puppy stops every once in a while and hops off the side of the trail into the tall grass and sniffs in circles, tail wagging.

There are eight of us and fifteen dogs and miles and miles of trails out in these fields behind the college, and it's making me think of what my grandma used to always say about finding happy places, places where you feel just right. And even if it's just Tuesdays and Fridays, out here with the Humane Society 7 and with Parker by my side is a happy place for me.

"Red!" Katherine calls back to us. "I'm naming her Red! She likes the red flowers and the red berries, and she keeps chewing on my red sneakers!" Then she and Red bound off down the path, and I can see this is her happy place too, and maybe it's not so bad to get attached.

When we bring the dogs back, I hand Max the end of Parker's leash, but I don't want to.

She pats my hand and looks right at me and says, "Cyrus, we're going to be shuffling some of the dogs around to other shelters to make some space. We're really at capacity."

If my dad were here, I'd look up at him so he could explain what *capacity* means, but she makes it sound like it means *too much* or *too hard*, and I'm wondering if they're getting too attached to him too.

"There's another humane society an hour from here that isn't full. Parker will join them there September ninth," she says. "Unless we find him a home."

Katherine holds tight to Red's leash and pats me on the back and I'm counting the days in my head and there's only one more walk day before the ninth. Friday. DeeDee puts her hand on my shoulder.

I nod to Max, but my heart hurts big achy hurts thinking about Parker being far away. After I say good-bye to The 7, I let Parker rest his nose on my shoulder for a whole minute before I tell him I have to go. "I'll see you Friday," I whisper.

Then I pinch my feet back into my cleats and run

down the sidewalk to the firehouse, blinking my eyes hard and trying not to think about September ninth and how Parker will be in a town I can't walk to and my happy place will be too far away for me to find.

I'm out of breath when I get to the firehouse, and Dad pinches his eyebrows together and gives me a look.

"Coach says if we're walking home we might as well run." I don't like how quickly the lie falls out of my mouth, but it's a good one because it sounds just like something Coach Matthews would say, and it makes my dad chuckle.

Sam slides down the pole and lands square on her feet. "Man, I love that," she says and smiles. "It just never gets old."

It reminds me of how Mr. Hewett leaned in when he talked to us and stood up to show us the pictures, and the way Marcus and Shane slam their chests together and chant *huh huh huh graaaa*, and how Chris describes flipping his canoe over his head and portaging from lake to lake in the Boundary Waters. And I try to come up with the things that make me smile wide like that. Listening to music with Grandma, especially when the horns join in. And Parker.

And now Parker is leaving.

Leo comes in the door and puts out his fist for a

pound. He and my dad bump knuckles and Leo claps me on the shoulder. "Quiet day?" he asks my dad.

"Prevention and inspection at the day cares," Dad says. I know what that looks like because I went along with them once. They check the alarms and teach the kids about stop, drop, and roll. They identify the exits and inspect for any hazardous materials. Then all the kids have a hundred questions that they ask all at the same time and everyone jumps up and down when my dad asks if they want to see the truck.

"I think I spotted a few future firefighters," Sam says. "That little girl in the front row with the wild curls and blue striped dress."

My dad nods his head and smirks, and I can tell he's recalling the little girl's face, and I'm thinking, great, another five-year-old who knows exactly what she loves.

Leo rolls his eyes and mumbles something about how it's hard to fit a dress under a pair of fireman's pants, and I wish he would take his hand off my shoulder.

"What was that?" Sam asks. "You were kind of mumbling."

"Nothing," he says. He takes his hand from my shoulder and waves it back and forth like he's trying to shoo Sam's question away, like he's trying to say *No big deal, forget it.*

But she doesn't forget it. "No, really," she says. "You

can say it out loud, in a big-boy voice."

That almost makes me laugh, but I look up at my dad first. His lips are pressed tight together, then he opens them and says, "Go ahead, Leo."

Leo just scoffs and shakes his head. "I'm going to get changed." Then he climbs the pole hand over hand and we hear locker number two slam upstairs.

Sam breaks into quiet chuckles and so does my dad, and I do too. "Big-boy voice," my dad says. "That was a good one."

Then Sam pats my shoulder, right where Leo clapped it earlier, and says, "Don't let anyone tell you where you do or don't fit."

On the way home I tell Dad all about the first day—about Mr. Hewett and how he read us a picture book, and how I already have an assignment due next week, and how we have a new kid with a really good memory. I leave out the parts about skipping practice and walking Parker. And I don't tell him that Shane was sent out of the circle and that Marcus wasn't very nice and that Mr. Hewett gave us a terrible look as if I were mumbling under my breath too.

Then I start wishing that Eduardo would speak up like Sam and not let Marcus and Shane and all the other kids giggle at him the way they do.

And that Marcus and Shane would quit acting the way they're acting and just go back to how they were when we played in Mighty-Mites and tossed a pee-wee-sized ball around our backyards.

And I wish I could speak up for Parker. Tell Max and everyone else that he doesn't want to leave and he'll be staying right here in Northfield, where the air smells like Cheerios and I can walk him every Tuesday and Friday forever.

CHAPTER 12

Team Spirit

In the morning, I pull my jersey over my head. It hangs down to my knees and looks more like a dress than a football uniform so I have to tuck it into my pants. When I stand in front of the mirror, my dad's number eighty-eight is folded over and half-buried beneath my elastic waist, so it looks like a big zero-zero across my front, which is about how I feel.

Dad tells me I look sharp and fast. But I've seen the picture of him in this uniform, and he didn't look like a zero-zero.

"Don't go breaking my record now," he says.

I tell him I can't make him any promises and that makes him chuckle and mess up my already messy hair.

"Meet at Grandma's after school," he reminds me.

I nod, grab my book bag, and head out the door toward school.

I know he's watching me again, so when I get to the corner I do that stop-and-catch-him thing again. And this time he doesn't duck down below the window and try to hide the fact that he's still got his eye on me. He just smiles a little half smile and raises his big hand, and it makes me feel a little less like a zero-zero.

As soon as I step into school, I hear cheering and see a bunch of maroon jerseys in a big huddle right there in the middle of the hallway like they're on the twenty-yard line. A few kids wearing soccer uniforms, an eighth-grade linebacker, and Marcus are at the center, and a bunch of other athletes are huddled around. Everyone else is gathering closer and cheering along, even the teachers.

"Give it a Heywood Hurrah!" the linebacker chants, and the rest of the team and everyone else responds.

"Heywood Hurrah! Heywood Hurrah!"

I spot Katherine, wearing her swim team T-shirt and a pair of goggles around her neck. Her hair is down and wet from morning practice, and she's pumping her fist. "Heywood Hurrah!" she shouts.

DeeDee shakes her head and smirks. She sees me through the crowd and rolls her eyes like this is the dumbest thing ever, but then she gives a little fist pump and mouths, *Heywood Hurrah!*

Before I can smile and roll my eyes back at her, two of the eighth graders from the huddle are grabbing me by the jersey and saying, "Come on, Olson!" and rushing me into the group and they're raising my fist in the air and we're all Heywood Hurrah–ing, and I immediately feel a little taller and a little more like eighty-eight than zero-zero.

Then I see Eduardo. He's wearing his book bag on his front again, and he's pumping his fist too and saying, "Give it a Heywood Hurrah!" He's springing over on his toes and trying to join our circle, but the defensemen keep bouncing him back out like he's a six-and-a-half-foot tight end trying to raid our end zone, and not the scrawniest kid in the school trying to cheer along with us.

Seeing them shove Eduardo off gives me that rock-in-the-gut feeling. I start to fake a coughing fit and point to the bathroom and try to wiggle out of the circle, but I keep getting nudged back to the middle, stuffed between all the shoulders and chanting. It's a lot harder getting out than it was getting pulled in by the jersey.

I close one eye and peek out between two linebackers and see Eduardo walk off, with his head down, toward Mr. Hewett's classroom.

When the bell rings, everyone hustles to their homerooms. Our huddle breaks up, but even when Mr. Hewett closes the door behind us, I can still hear the echoes of a Heywood Hurrah down the hallway.

There's a color-printed picture of *Calvin Can't Fly* stapled to the bulletin board beneath the *Classroom Book a Day* sign, and my stomach relaxes a little thinking maybe that counts, a picture book we read together, because that's something I can do.

Before anything else, Mr. Hewett tells us that today we're getting our lockers. We all say, "Yes!"

"In the sixth grade, you get to share with a locker buddy." The way he says it makes sharing sound awesome.

Right away I see Marcus and Shane crash their shoulders into each other and say, "Locker buddies!" They stand side by side in their Heywood uniforms. Everyone else is moving toward a buddy, and in a few seconds the whole class is standing two by two around the room. Zander is standing with Benji, and Nora's with Emily. Patrick is moving over toward Geordie, who almost never talks, and gesturing like they could be good locker buddies.

There are only two people left alone: Eduardo and

me. He smiles and says, "I guess we're locker buddies."

Marcus muscles over quick between us and yanks me by the zero-zero. "Wait a second. Mr. Hewett, can we have three in our locker group? We don't mind squeezing in."

Eduardo looks down at his Velcro shoes and Shane says, "Yeah, we can share with Cyrus." We stand three in a row like we're getting ready to attack the end zone.

I'm waiting for Mr. Hewett to say no and make me go back to sharing with Eduardo because it feels like Marcus and Shane are being more mean to Eduardo than nice to me, and that's what teachers are for: stopping kids from being mean. But he doesn't say anything. Instead, he's looking at me. He's looking deep down to my queasy stomach where the right thing to do is flipping and flopping around, and he's waiting. Waiting for me to tell Marcus and Shane that I'd rather share with Eduardo. Waiting for me to do the right thing. Everyone else is quieting too, and looking at me, because they want to get into the hallway already to start unpacking and decorating their new lockers.

I open my mouth, but nothing comes out. I try to say that it's OK, I'll stick with Eduardo. I really do, but I'm just silent. My cheeks get hot.

Mr. Hewett points to a few pairs of locker buddies

and says they can go choose their lockers first. They rush out the door, and Marcus and Shane sigh and say, "Come on already, Cy."

Eduardo is still looking at his shoes.

"I—I . . . It doesn't matter to me," I say.

Then I think of the lockers at the firehouse and how Leo made a big stink about getting locker number two and how ridiculous he sounded and how I was thinking the whole time, it's just a locker. And I'm guessing that if Leo were me, he'd go with Marcus and Shane faster than it takes to slide down the pole in a five-alarm fire.

Mr. Hewett gives me three more seconds to say something, and just as he's about to tell me what to do, I blurt, "Actually, I'll buddy with Eduardo."

Eduardo looks at me and says, "Well, I could have used the extra space, but I guess being your buddy is fine too." He says it with a big smile that spills into a giggle and makes me laugh with him.

Marcus rolls his eyes and I stuff my laugh away and kind of shrug my shoulders at them like I'm taking one for the team this time, and that makes my stomach get uneasy-queasy all over again.

Mr. Hewett dismisses the rest of the pairs to the hallway to get their lockers, except Marcus and Shane. "You guys can wait," he says. They argue that that's not fair and sigh and slam their book bags on the table and

I'm wondering what happened to them because they were never-slam-your-book-bag kind of people.

Eduardo and I choose the locker closest to Mr. Hewett's room and we divide it in half.

"I'll take the bottom. I'm tiny," he says and sits right down on the floor on his knees like he's a kindergartener. He takes a Ninja Turtles magnet out of his book bag and sticks a picture way down on the inside of the door. In the picture, a boy who stands a whole head taller than Eduardo, with wide football shoulders, a little darker skin, and long hair pulled up in a bun on top of his head has his arm around Eduardo. The picture looks old, but Eduardo looks exactly the same.

He catches me glancing. "First day of fourth grade," he says.

"Is that your—"

"Twin," he says. "I know, I know. He looks nothing like me and three years older. But actually, I'm two minutes older than he is."

I bend down and sit on my knees too to get a closer look. "Your twin?" I ask.

"Alejandro," he tells me. "He's in Ms. Freeman's homeroom."

I want to ask him one hundred more questions. Like why didn't his brother try out for football? And do they get along? And why haven't I seen him yet? And where did they live before this year? And how can they be twins and look so different?

But Mr. Hewett is opening the door and letting Marcus and Shane out to pick the last locker, the one with the handle that sticks unless you wiggle it hard, and calling us all back to the room.

When we get in from the hallway, Mr. Hewett asks us to come over to the rug area and he's holding another picture book.

"Seriously?" Marcus mutters.

I fake that I have to tie my shoelaces and let Marcus and Shane go ahead and sit in the back corner of Mr. Hewett's purple reading rug. Benji, Chris, and Zander fill in around them and stick their legs out long, leaning back on their hands, and the only space wide enough on the crammed rug even for my skinny little frame is right between the edge and Eduardo.

He pats the spot with his hand and scooches over, inviting me to sit.

Marcus snickers, but I pretend I don't hear and sit down.

"Thanks," I whisper.

Mr. Hewett holds up another picture book and I hear lots of giggles behind me and a few big huffy sighs. Eduardo does a small little fist pump behind the book bag on his chest and whispers, "Yes!" just loud enough for me to hear. That's how I'm feeling too.

"Are we going to read a picture book every day?" Hadleigh asks.

"Now, isn't that a great idea!" Mr. Hewett responds, and he sounds serious and excited and like maybe he had that plan all along. Everyone calls out, "No, no, no," and, "Hadleeeeeeeigh," like she just gave him this idea and now we're going to have to suffer a zillion more picture books because of her.

Mr. Hewett doesn't even wait for the class to quiet down; he just starts right in reading and everyone kind of stops talking and moaning and listens, because I think deep down every one of us actually wants to hear the story, and maybe Mr. Hewett is like Grandma and can see that far into all our secrets.

I hope not.

The main character of the book's name is Ramón, and Mr. Hewett knows how to pronounce it so the *R* rolls and the *ó* hammers down hard. The way Milly sounds when she calls me *muchacho*. The way Eduardo sounds when he says his own name.

Ramón's big brother laughs at his drawings, so he crumples them and gives up on art. But Ramón has a little sister whose name is Marisol, which sounds so good when Mr. Hewett says it that I wish he would read the whole book over again as soon as it's done. Marisol collects all the crumpled drawings and hangs them in her room and tells Ramón that drawings don't have to be perfect to be beautiful. They can be *ish*. So Ramón draws a fish-*ish* and an afternoon-*ish* and then he starts to write poetry-*ish*.

It's hard to explain, but I just like the way this book sounds. Not only how the names roll off Mr. Hewett's tongue, but also the repetition of *ish ish ish* and the way it feels light and easy at the end, like I could float away on the last page and not have to worry about being *good* at anything ever.

Eduardo raises his hand and asks, "*Habla español?*"

Mr. Hewett smiles and nods his head. "*Sí. Hablo español-ish.*"

"*Tiene un buen acento.*"

Marcus humphs and mumbles something about gibber-*ish* beneath his breath and a few kids laugh. Mr. Hewett stops talking with Eduardo and gives Marcus a look like he better quit it. Marcus says, "My bad," but he doesn't look like he means it.

When everyone is getting up from the rug, Eduardo leans over and whispers, "I can teach you a few words if you want."

When he says it, Marcus and Shane are staring right at me in their matching maroon Heywood jerseys. I pretend not to hear Eduardo, and when I stand up to return to my table in the back of the room I can feel how long and heavy my jersey hangs.

Mr. Hewett tells us that instead of going to first-period science class, the whole sixth grade is going to the auditorium for a presentation from the band teacher.

"Band?" Shane asks. "We have to be in band?"

"It's voluntary," Mr. Hewett says. "It meets Monday, Tuesday, and Friday after school. I know because they practice right above my room." He points to the ceiling and it makes us laugh. "Mr. Fletcher will tell you everything you need to know about how to sign up, and then he'll give you a little demonstration of each instrument."

I see Eduardo's shoulders jump when he hears that, and I'm pretty sure he did another one of those fist pumps under his book bag again.

"The A Team has practice anyway," Marcus says loud enough for everyone to hear.

Addison calls out, "What if I want to play soccer and be in the band?"

Mr. Hewett shrugs and says he's sorry, and that we might have to make some tough decisions. "Just keep your ears and minds open in the assembly. You'll know what to do."

He leans *Ish* in the tray of the chalkboard next to *Calvin Can't Fly.*

The bell rings and we all start packing up.

Through all the chairs dragging across the floor, I hear Nora say to Emily, "I'm going to play the flute. You should too so we can sit next to each other." I hear Chris and Geordie talking about the drums.

Marcus is the first to the door, but before he opens it Mr. Hewett raises his voice over us and says, "Don't decide your instrument right now. See if any get your foot tapping. Then choose."

Our class is the first one there. We walk through the big double doors to the auditorium and file into the first row. I'm sitting between Eduardo and Marcus and looking at all the instruments on the stage. I don't know the names of a lot of them, but my eyes get caught on the silver and brass ones that look complicated with buttons and tubes that twist around big horns. And I wonder how breath can travel through all of those bends and turns and make the squealing surges that blare from Grandma's records.

Eduardo sits up on his knees and leans forward like he's been waiting for this. Then someone taps him on the shoulder and I turn to see the boy from the picture. He still wears his long hair in a bun on top of his head, but he seems even taller now than in the picture.

Eduardo turns and smiles bigger than I've seen before and they speak quick words back and forth in

Spanish. He introduces me and I say hi.

"Hi," Alejandro says. "Eduardo told me you like dogs."

I smile and say, "He did? Yeah, I do."

Onstage, Mr. Fletcher unsnaps another big music case and pulls out two parts of an instrument. He starts putting them together into a long shiny round slide that I've seen move back and forth in the parades at Defeat of Jesse James Days.

Then he taps the microphone and starts telling us about the Joseph Lee Heywood band. He's going on about how you don't have to know anything about music to join and learn and he encourages us all to listen and then talk it over with our parents.

"The returning seventh and eighth graders will play this weekend at the Defeat of Jesse James Days football game. We play at many of the sporting games to boost team spirit," he tells us. "Because nothing lifts us up like a good beat."

Then Mr. Fletcher hands a stack of forms to the kids sitting at the ends of rows and tells us to each take one and pass it.

"There's a list of instruments on the back," he says. "I'll demonstrate each one. You can take notes about what you hear and what you like." He turns the form back over. "If you decide you want to join the band, fill in your instrument of choice and have your parent sign. First rehearsal is Friday."

Then he picks up a guitar that's plugged into a big amp and strums the strings. Everyone starts cheering, and then they cheer even louder for the drums.

I see Nora and Emily draw big hearts around the word *flute* on the backs of their forms.

Mr. Fletcher keeps moving down the line of instruments. He tells us what a tuba is and an oboe. And I even like the way the names of the instruments sound. And every time he starts to play, he taps his foot and says, "One-and-two-and-three-and-four-and." I like the way that sounds too.

But when he picks up the long slide and tells us, "This is a trombone," then, "One-and-two-and-three-and-four-and," and starts buzzing his lips in the mouthpiece and gliding his arm out and back and that *whaawooo!* comes out of the horn, something happens, and it feels more like team spirit than wearing the same jersey and huddling up for a Heywood Hurrah. It feels like the music's coming straight in my body through my ears and pressing on my lungs and beating with my heart and gliding all the way down to my feet and making my toes tap too, like Mr. Fletcher's, like Grandma's, and with the notes climbing up the slide and blaring out the horn, it feels like this is right where I belong.

I see Marcus looking over at me, so I try to ease the smile off my face and keep my body from bouncing along with the rhythm too much. But then Mr. Fletcher makes the sound go way down low, then scream back up the slide to a high, long sing. He lets the sound fall again, the notes tumbling down the slide. And when I look down at my scaredy-skateboard-braking-worn Vans, I see they're tapping harder than ever, and I think they might even be tapping right on beat.

Eduardo points to my shoes and says, "Seems like you've got your answer."

I shake my head. "I can't play that."

Mr. Fletcher does one more long slide—*whaawoo!*— and puts the trombone down, and Eduardo looks at me again.

"Maybe you could play-*ish*."

That makes me smile. "I have football practice on Tuesdays and Fridays," I say. Eduardo looks at me and kind of shrugs, and even though I don't really know Eduardo, I think I know what he's saying. I think he's saying *Sorry*.

On the way out of the auditorium, Marcus and Shane crumple up their forms and toss them into the garbage. Eduardo folds his twice and slides it into his pocket. I look back at the stage, and Mr. Fletcher is taking apart the trombone and putting the big pieces into the velvet-lined case. I can still hear the *whaawooo!* sliding down and up, and it makes me walk different. Like *one-and-two-and-three-and-four-and.*

On our way out of the auditorium, I crumple the form and toss it in the garbage can with the others who won't be joining band.

CHAPTER 13

Finding X

When I get to Grandma's after school, a woman is playing the piano in the lobby and Grandma is there sitting on the end of the couch. Her right hand is tucked in tight to her side, where it always is, but her left hand is floating in the air in front of her like she's conducting, moving up and down and left and right in four perfect beats over and over, like Mr. Fletcher's *one-and-two-and-three-and-four-and*. Her eyes are closed, and even though the right side of her mouth turns down, I can tell she's smiling. And her left foot is tapping. Tapping right on beat.

I sit down next to her and pat her left knee.

She grabs my hand but doesn't open her eyes. "Na na," she whispers, and I know she's saying *Cyrus*, that she knows it's me and she's glad I'm here. Her hand squeezes mine. We call this giving strength in my family, when you take a tired, scared hand in your own and squeeze it tight until all your strength flows over.

I gave my grandma strength every day we visited her in the hospital after she had her stroke, and my dad gave me strength every night when we returned home and he tucked me into bed, both of us hoping that Grandma's words would return tomorrow.

I can feel Grandma's strength filling me up, and I don't know how she knows I need it, but I do know that before the song is over and she opens her eyes, both of our left feet are tapping together.

Milly delivers dinner to us in Grandma's apartment, and there are two extra brownies on my tray. She gives me a wink.

There's a Twins game on mute and a record playing and Grandma is cutting fish with her fork in her left hand. I want to reach over and do it for her, but I don't know how to help without making her feel like a little kid. The fish is crispy on one side, and she can't get the fork through. She spears it and tries to shake it free, but the whole piece of fish lifts up and some of it falls down her shirt.

"Na!" she shouts and slams her fork to the plate.

I move closer and put my right hand on her left and give it a little strength while I count out a beat of *one-and-two-and-three-and-four-and* over and over, and with my hand I'm telling her to slow down and it's OK. Slow down and try again.

She takes the fish from her shirt and puts it back on her plate. Then she tries again, slower this time, edging her fork back and forth through the crispy part until it breaks through and she cheers, "Na na na!"

She finishes the rest on her own, going more slowly like I showed her, and I eat all the brownies by the second inning.

"I should have saved one for Dad."

Grandma shakes her head and waves me off and says, "Na na na," and it gets us both laughing because I know she's saying *Our secret*.

Then she points to my book bag and makes the zipping motion. She wants to see my schoolwork.

"I don't really have much yet, Grandma." But she keeps pointing, so I open it up and take out my graph paper notebook and show her some problems we worked on together in class. I'm OK at math, especially at balancing equations and finding X.

I tell Grandma that I like my new math teacher, Ms.

Martin, because she pulled out little scales and a bucket of different-sized blocks to practice balancing equations. "What goes on one side has to go on the other," she said. "And what comes off one side, has to come off the other. You have to keep it balanced." She let us play with the scales for a while and it didn't even feel like school. Then we did some problems together on the board and she drew an equation to look like a scale and it all just clicked and made sense.

Not like reading.

Grandma reaches her hand in and takes out my English folder and Mr. Hewett's assignment. She reads it and raises her eyebrows at me. "Na na?" she asks, and I know she's saying *Which book?*

I shrug. "Not sure yet."

I flip a page in my graph paper notebook and show her how I did this equation by myself and found X in three steps and Ms. Martin wrote a little note—*I like the way your brain works!*—in pink pen right in the middle of class. Grandma gives me a high five, but then she pulls *Wonder* out of my bag. She taps her finger on the cover.

"Haven't started it yet."

She taps again. "Na." And I know she's saying *Now. No time like the present*, because that's something my grandma always used to say.

She turns to the first page, holds the cover open with her left hand, and passes it to me. And even though it's supposed to be Grandma reading to me, and I miss her voice and the way it rose and fell across the pages, I can do this. So I start reading out loud to Grandma, and before I realize it I'm on the third page and Grandma is tapping her hand on mine, telling me to stop a second.

"Na na na." And I know she's saying *beautiful* because I didn't skip any words or stumble at all.

Then she leans over and points to the word *August*.

"August," I read.

Grandma curls her left hand to say *And . . .* or *Tell me more*, and I try to quickly read the sentence before it and after it in my head again so I can tell her more about August, but nothing is sticking and even though I read the pages perfectly I don't know what I read and it feels panicky like the one time I tried sliding down the pole at the firehouse because it looked so easy, but I didn't know how to use my legs like they do and the pole just kept slipping and burning between my fingers and I didn't have anything to hold on to.

When I look up at Grandma and try my best fake, "This is a book about summer," it feels like I'm crashing hard to the floor after a scary free fall.

She smiles her half smile and takes the book from my hands. "Na na na na na na na." But I don't know what she's saying, so I start asking questions.

"You've read this book?" I ask. She shakes her head, so I try again.

"You want me to read the whole book and tell you what it's about next time I come over? I can do that, Grandma." But she shakes her head again and makes gestures with her hands and I just can't figure it out. I can't read Grandma right now either.

"Na na na na na na!"

"You want to see more of my math homework?"

"Na!" She smacks her palm on the hard cover of *Wonder*, and I can see tears forming at the corner of her eyes. She puts her head back in her chair and for a second I think maybe she's frustrated and tired and she'll fall asleep before Dad even gets here to pick me up.

Then she takes a deep breath and taps the cover soft with her finger with that same rhythm. *One-and-two-and-three-and-four-and.* Then she lifts her hand into the air and moves it like she did when we were listening to the piano music in the lobby, like she's conducting. *One-and-two-and-three-and-four-and.*

And now I know what she's saying. She's saying slow down and try again, just like I was telling her when she was trying to cut her fish. I go to take the book from her lap so I can try again, slower this time, but she slaps her hand down on the book and holds on tight to the cover. "Na na na na na." Then she leans back and closes her eyes again. She tap-tap-taps on the book cover and starts conducting again, *one-and-two-and-three-and-four-and*, and I'm thinking that she might be saying something else.

After a few beats, she turns to me and looks right into my eyes and right down deep to where my secret is, and she smiles her half smile that says *It's OK*. She opens the book to the first page and sings the first sentence to me, her finger running across each word. "Na na na na na na na na na." Then she stops and sways and closes her eyes and uses her left hand to conduct an imaginary orchestra in the air. Then she sings the second sentence. "Na na na na na na." She stops and sways again before she taps the third sentence hard with her finger and says each word like a punch. "Na na na."

I'm following along with all the words, and when my grandma stops to sway I know what she's saying. Slow down. Rest. Wait. Think. Each sentence has its own rhythm.

I read each sentence with my grandma conducting, stopping and swaying when she does and thinking about each sentence before I go on. So when we get to *August*, she stops and points and looks right at me, her eyebrows up in a question.

"August is the character," I say. "He likes ice cream and feels normal, but for some reason other people don't think he is." And when I tell her that, it doesn't feel like falling down the firehouse pole, it feels like finding X.

"Na na na na!" she cheers. And I'm pretty sure she's giving me a Heywood Hurrah.

Dad opens the door, and Grandma pretends she's not happy to see him because when he comes that means it's time for me to go.

Grandma hands me the book, and I zip it into my bag with my graph paper notebook. She pulls me into a big hug with her left hand. "Na na na," she whispers in my ear, and at first I think she's trying to remind me to listen to each sentence, to sing it before I rush on, but when I pull away and look at her and see the smile spreading out in little wrinkles from the corners of her eyes, I know she's saying that the three brownies I ate after dinner will stay our little secret. And I know they will. Grandma's good at holding secrets.

That night, I sit on my bed with *Wonder* open to the page that Grandma folded down like a dog ear, and that makes me think of Parker. Grandma and I didn't get too far in the book, but it's the first time I can actually remember what I read and I don't have to start all over.

There are a lot of words on each page, but the chapters are short, so I feel like I can get to the next one if I just keep going like Grandma showed me. Sentence by sentence.

I hold my finger out just like she did and point to each word, and under my breath I say them all and stop at each period and sway like Grandma did, back and forth, finding the rhythm and thinking. Sometimes the sentences are long and I have to take a breath at the commas before I finish, and sometimes the sentences are short and easy to say and remember all in one breath.

The character, Auggie, is telling the story of how when he was born the doctor fainted because of the way his face looked, and even though I remember reading with Grandma that he had lots of surgeries, I don't know exactly what is wrong with his face. Then he tells about a farting nurse in the delivery room and even though I'm wondering if there are any stories from my birth and who knows them, it makes me laugh so loud that Dad comes in.

"What's so funny?"

I look up from the page. "This book Grandma got me."

He smiles and taps the door frame with his big hand before he leaves. "Good."

And because I'm OK at math I know that if I read *Wonder* at this rate it'll take me thirty-nine days to finish. But even so, it feels like running through the trails with Parker. Free.

CHAPTER 14

Sissy

Nora and Emily come into Mr. Hewett's class together giggling and holding their permissions slips to join band. "Flute!" they sing. Chris is banging the edge of his desk. "Drum solo!" he shouts and dings his pencils off his fancy hiking water bottle and across his books and ends with banging the back of his chair so hard that one of the pencils breaks.

Mr. Hewett says he's glad people are excited about the band and reminds us that our slips are due tomorrow to Mr. Fletcher if we're interested. Marcus scoffs and mumbles under his breath, something about how the cool people are on the field, not in the band. I pretend I can't hear him and start looking around the classroom. A color-printed picture of *Ish* is next to

Calvin Can't Fly on the bulletin board, and I wonder what we'll read today.

Mr. Hewett says that instead of coming to the rug area for a read-aloud, we're going to get in groups of three or four and read aloud to one another. He hands us each a stapled packet of copy paper with the title *Oliver Button Is a Sissy* across the front page.

"This is a typed-up copy," he tells us. "But I have the real version up here so you can see the pictures after if you want."

The whole class is starting to drag chairs and make little groups. I'm already sitting in the back with Marcus and Shane and they're writing their names on the tops of their packets and I guess we're just going to be a group.

Patrick and Curtis get up from Eduardo's table in the front and join Joel and Benji. Eduardo starts looking around to see where he could add in, and I look away fast, not because I don't want to be in his group, but I don't want him to be with Marcus and Shane because being in the middle of them makes me feel all icky-itchy-queasy.

But I'm not quick enough. Eduardo catches my eye and motions to the empty seat next to me. I give a little nod while Marcus and Shane still have their heads down, and Eduardo makes his way over.

"Uh-oh," Shane mumbles. "Here comes Ed*weird*o."

I pretend I don't hear and my throat closes a little.

"Room for one more?" Eduardo pulls out the chair, sits down, and starts writing his name on top of his packet too.

Marcus and Shane don't say anything, but I see Marcus roll his eyes.

Mr. Hewett tells us to take turns reading and he'll stop by our tables to listen in.

Marcus juts his chin out toward Eduardo. "You read."

"I'd be happy to go first!" he replies, and I wish he wouldn't sound so excited about reading a picture book out loud because it makes Marcus snort and Shane pretend to push a pair of glasses up his nose.

And I think maybe I should bang my fist down hard on the table and tell them to stop, but Eduardo starts reading. It's about a boy named Oliver Button who likes to play dress-up and paper dolls and sing, but I'm thinking more about the way Eduardo's reading, with a voice that goes up and down like he's performing onstage, and I'm thinking about the little snickers I'm hearing from people looking over at our table, and I'm wondering why Eduardo is jotting little underlines and notes on his paper as he reads. I'm flipping the pages and even though I'm OK at following along when others read, I'm not really paying attention because I'm too focused on who's making fun of Eduardo.

Then he stops and says, "Someone else's turn."

Marcus is hiding a laugh and Shane is leaning back with his arms folded across his chest, so I say I'll go. Eduardo points to where he left off and I say thanks and start reading. But not the way Grandma showed me, tapping my finger across the words and swaying after each sentence until it settles in me. I'm reading fast and it sounds good and I'm on a roll when Mr. Hewett sits down at our table.

I read the words *girls* and *sissy* and Marcus laughs and I'm not really keeping up with the story, so I laugh too because that's a good fake, following other people's reactions. And the whole time Eduardo keeps jotting little notes on his pages.

At the end, Mr. Hewett tells me that that was some mighty fine reading and it makes me smile. "What is one thing that stands out to you from this story?" he asks.

He's asking the table, but I know I'm off the hook because I did the reading. That's one of my best fakes. Eduardo looks at Marcus and Shane and I do too because it's their turn to talk, but they just look right back at me with eyes that say *You talk* and before I have a chance to flip back through the pages and practice a response in my head that might fit with the story, Mr. Hewett says,

"Cyrus? What about you? What's one thing that stands out to you?"

"I—I . . ." My fingers turn the pages in front of me, and I try to move just my eyeballs over to Eduardo's pages to see if I can read a note he jotted, but his handwriting is too small. And before I know it, I'm looking at the big title across the top of the first page and saying, "Oliver is the main character and he's a sissy."

Marcus and Shane hoot right out loud and Eduardo barks, "What?"

Mr. Hewett doesn't even say I'm wrong, which feels worse because I know I am. Instead he asks, "What makes you say that?" And I can't think of one single thing and now everyone is looking at our table and I can feel my face getting hot and the words on the page are turning blurry.

"C-can I go to the bathroom?" I blurt.

I hear more laughter but I don't wait to see where it's coming from and I don't wait for Mr. Hewett to say OK. I just bolt out the door and down the hall, past my dad's picture in the trophy case, and into the bathroom.

I close the stall door and try not to cry and I'm thinking about how I can get out of here and back into class without everyone laughing and without Mr. Hewett wondering why I couldn't answer such a simple question.

I need a good fake.

I could tell him I was zoning out the whole time I was reading because I was thinking about the Vikings or the Twins, or that I didn't sleep well last night. I could tell him I was actually thinking about this other book I'm reading and that I'm worried about Auggie starting at a new school because I know there's something really different about the way his face looks and I'm pretty sure kids will laugh at him.

But thinking about *Wonder* makes the tears sneak down my cheeks. Maybe because I don't want anyone to laugh at Auggie. Maybe because I'm not sure if I can ever read like that again. That even if I try the exact way that Grandma showed me, the farther I get past page eight the less and less I'll be able to do it, even if I *na na na* with my finger through each sentence slowly, swaying and thinking and trying. I'll get lost and I'll give up and I'll have to search the internet to find out if Auggie is OK.

For one minute I think that I'll just skip the rest of the day—I'll open the bathroom door, look left and right, and make a break for it. I'll run all the way to the humane society, where I can park my head right on Parker's shoulder even though it's not a Tuesday or Friday.

But then the school would call my dad, and he'd have to worry and wonder and I'd have to come up with more fakes about where I was and why I left school. And I think I'd rather open the door to Mr. Hewett's classroom than hear my dad explain, again, how he was so worried about me.

So I wipe my eyes and open the bathroom door and walk down the hallway slowly, back to Mr. Hewett's room. When I go in, a few people look up, then back down quickly and pretend to be discussing the questions stapled to the back of *Oliver Button Is a Sissy*. I can tell Mr. Hewett said something to them while I was gone about how to not make my awkward meltdown a big deal and to welcome me back kindly. Emily looks up and sort of smiles, and Geordie juts his chin out like he's saying *What's up, Cy?*

When I sit back down at my table Eduardo looks right at my eyes and says, "You OK?" And I can tell he's not saying it because Mr. Hewett told him to be nice. He would have said that no matter what.

"Yeah," I whisper.

Marcus reaches out for a fist bump, and that makes me feel really good until he says, "Don't worry about anything, Cy. You were right on. Oliver Button *is* kind of a sissy." Shane's nodding along, and out of the corner of my eye I can see Eduardo shaking his head.

I want to say something, but I don't know what actually happened in the story, and I can feel my throat closing before I can get any words up and out.

I hear Addison and Hadleigh at the table behind me saying that just because Oliver doesn't do sports doesn't mean he's a sissy, and that it's cool that he likes to dance.

"Guys need to know how to dance too!" Addison says.

"Right?" says Hadleigh.

Benji leans his chair back on two legs and butts into the conversation at their table. "But *tap*-dance?" he says, and makes a big deal about fluttering his lashes. Addison rolls her eyes at him and Hadleigh pushes his chair back down.

"No one asked you."

And that reminds me of Sam and the way she talks right back to Leo, and it makes me want to say something even more, but before I can clear my throat Eduardo says, "He is not. He's not a sissy."

That makes Marcus and Shane laugh, and Shane says, "Of course *you'd* think that." Mr. Hewett is sitting across the room at Geordie, Chris, and Zander's table, but he stands right up and gives us all the look. The look he gave on the first day that makes me feel guilty just for sitting next to them.

The bell rings, and we start packing our bags, and Mr. Hewett is reminding us that our Best Book Ever review is due next week and to be thinking about it. We'll spend some time on it in class, but we're expected to work at home too.

I fake that I have to tie my shoe and let Marcus and Shane leave first. "I'll catch up," I tell them.

When I lean down to fiddle with my laces, I can see they're kind of waiting for me just outside the door to walk to math class. I hear Marcus say, "Eduardo Button is a sissy," and he sounds so stupid because Eduardo's last name isn't Button, it's Gutierrez with rolling *r*s that they could never pronounce. Shane laughs and sprays a sip of soda that he isn't supposed to be drinking in school. Kids passing by say, "Ewwww," and, "Gross." That makes him laugh and spray more, and they both wave for me to come on. My stomach jumps, but before my throat can close up again I say, "That's OK. Go ahead without me. I'll walk with Eduardo."

Shane slowly spins the top back on his soda bottle, and Marcus scoffs and laughs and pulls the straps on his book bag tighter. "Fine." Then they walk off.

Eduardo smiles and closes his notebook. I can see the signed band permission slip sticking out from the back pages. He catches me looking and gestures a long slide of the trombone and lifts his eyebrows in a question.

I shake my head no. "Football," I say. And he shrugs his shoulders.

But just watching Eduardo gesture the slide of the

trombone makes notes tap inside me.

On the way out, he asks Mr. Hewett if he can borrow the real version of *Oliver Button Is a Sissy*, the one with the pictures that's leaning in the chalkboard tray next to the others. He tucks it under his arm and says, "Let's go."

When we get to math class, I'm a little scared to see how Marcus and Shane will look at me, but moving down the hall to the music beating in my guts, next to Eduardo, feels like right where I belong.

Eduardo flips the pages of the picture book beneath our table while I'm busy finding X. I glance down at the book when Ms. Martin is on the other side of the room helping Geordie balance blocks on his algebra scale. And with just one picture I can see why kids were calling Oliver Button a sissy. He stands by himself with a handful of flowers while three boys in football uniforms tackle each other in the background. And even though I don't care much about flowers, I'm thinking that I'd rather be picking daffodils than crashing helmets. But I'm not brave like that. Brave like sit-out-of-football-practice-to-make-a-bouquet brave. Brave like Oliver Button brave.

CHAPTER 15

Type O

When I get to the firehouse parking lot after school, I see a big sign stretched above the door. *Blood Drive Today.*

Leo is hauling two big trash bags to the Dumpster in the lot. "No practice today?"

I shake my head and say, "B Team is Tuesday and Friday."

"Well, that's not enough, is it?" he asks. "I can train you on the other days. Touch-and-goes and bench presses, and you watch, Coach will want to move you up to the A Team before October."

I nod my head and say, "Yeah, maybe." But really, no. Then I open the door right where I was left as a screaming baby and right where Parker whimpered until we let him in.

This is the first time the firehouse is hosting a blood drive, and the whole first floor has big lounge chairs and nurses and stations for each volunteer. I try not to look too hard at anything because I don't like needles or blood.

My dad is checking people in, handing them clipboards and pens so they can fill out paperwork. He nods to me and says he'll be another hour or so, but I can do my homework upstairs or help out.

Sam's in the kitchen pouring juice into little paper cups and handing sliced bagels to people with white gauze and Band-Aids stuck in the crooks of their arms. She introduces herself to everyone and says she's the new firefighter here. I'm watching all their faces and waiting to see how they react to a woman in a firehouse T-shirt and suspenders. Most people smile and reach out a hand to shake. Mr. Watson, who plows our driveway after every snowstorm, hesitates a little, but says, "Well, welcome to Northfield!"

I watch them all as they walk away too, to see if anyone scoffs or rolls their eyes behind Sam's back like Leo does. But they don't. And I'm glad.

Dr. Davis, who's been my doctor forever and taught Dad everything he needed to know about car seats and infant formula, says, "Let me go get my daughter! She'd love to meet you, Sam," and hurries off to find her six-year-old.

I recognize most everyone. Professor Laird is here. He was my grandma's neighbor up on College Street before she had her stroke and moved into her assisted-living development. And Eunice owns the coffee shop on Division Street where college kids sit all day, jotting little notes in textbooks like Eduardo did all over *Oliver Button Is a Sissy.*

A few people say, "Hey, Cyrus," and ask how middle school is going. I smile and say it's pretty good.

"I'll see you Saturday," Professor Laird says. "About time we got another Olson on the team!" He puts his arm around my shoulders and gives me a good shake.

I tell him I'm just on the B Team and I won't actually be playing in the Defeat of Jesse James Days game, and he says that doesn't matter one bit.

Leo comes back in and puts new garbage bags in the bins.

Sam calls him over and hands him a tray. "Let's offer some juice to the blood donors."

Leo takes the tray, and I can tell his hands are shaking because the juice in the little cups is sloshing from side to side. "I . . . uh . . . Don't you think we should keep the juice in the kitchen? I don't want them spilling." He sets the tray down and says he has to go to the bath-room, which sounds to me an awful lot like a fake.

Sam looks at me and shrugs like *What was that?* I shrug too.

Roger says that Leo's being ridiculous and takes the tray to pass out the juice. Dad pokes his head in and tells me that all the firefighters are giving blood before they leave, and I'm so glad that I'm not 110 pounds or sixteen years old because I know giving blood is a good thing to do but I can hardly stomach a finger prick with Dr. Davis.

Roger passes out the last cup, returns the tray to the kitchen, and joins Dad and Sam at the back of the line and starts filling out paperwork to donate.

Leo slides back down the pole and starts heading toward the kitchen. My dad is trying to get his attention, but Leo isn't looking in that direction at all.

"Leo!" my dad calls, and I can tell Leo is faking that he doesn't hear and trying to busy himself in the kitchen with throwing out paper cups and plates and organizing the leftover bagels.

I tap him on the shoulder. "My dad wants to talk to you," I say, pointing through all the volunteers with their arms out straight and blood slowly filling bags hanging from tall, silver poles.

"Get in line!" my dad hollers. "We're last, then clos-ing up."

He points at himself like *Me?* and my dad says, "Yeah, you." Leo sighs and walks slowly over and I'm kind of feeling bad for him, even though he's been pretty rotten lately, because it stinks when your fake doesn't work and you have to do something you don't know how to do.

A nurse calls Dad to a chair, then another calls Sam. Roger is already done and getting his Band-Aid and walking back to the kitchen to get a bagel.

"Your turn, sir," the nurse says and waves Leo over. He sits down, and the nurse wraps a wide blue rubber band around his big bicep and taps her gloved fingers on his veins. Then she pulls out a long needle. Leo starts talking really fast and telling her how much he can bench-press and how many pull-ups he can do with weighted ankles. And it's like just talking about the exercises is making him sweat, because I can see it on his face from here and he's breathing hard and wiping his forehead.

"Sir?" The nurse looks at the paperwork on the clip-board. "Mr. Mason?" Leo doesn't respond. She snaps her fingers in front of his face. "I'm going to help you put your head between your knees, sir."

Then she swings his legs over the side of the chair and guides his head between his knees, holding on to his suspender straps. "Can you hear me?" After a minute, Leo shakes his head and says he's fine, he's fine, he's fine. But the nurse makes him lie back on the chair and cranks his feet way up high.

Dad and Sam finish filling their bags and get gauze stuck in the crooks of their arms, then they go over to Leo's chair and Roger brings him a cup of juice. The nurse checks Leo's pulse and assures everyone that he's OK. "Just a little woozy around needles is all," she says. "Did you all not know that?" She looks up at my dad and Roger and Sam, who are surrounding his chair and looking down at him.

My dad shakes his head. "I didn't." Then his shoulders start to bump up and down, and I know that means he's trying to hold in a laugh, but he just can't. And I can't either because I'm thinking about Leo's big muscles bulging as he touch-and-goes across the gym mats upstairs and pulls himself up the firehouse pole with just his arms. And how his big muscles didn't matter one little bit when the nurse pulled out the needle.

"I'm not scared," Leo sputters. "I just didn't eat lunch and I had a big workout this morning."

"OK, Leo," Roger says and pats his shoulder.

Leo's hand shakes a little as he takes the juice from

Sam and his face is turning from white as a sheet to fire-engine red. "I'm fine," he says, and he starts to get up even though the nurse says to give it a minute.

Everyone else has left, and the nurses are starting to pack up their stations and transport everything out to the vans with the big red crosses on the side. Leo is finishing his juice and going through the bag of leftover bagels until he finds a cinnamon raisin.

Dad's about to change his clothes and get ready to lock up so we can go home when there's a quick, loud knock and a woman pushes through the big firehouse front door. "Are we too late?" she huffs. A girl follows her, and the wind blows in a few leaves behind them before they shut the door. "Shoot, we're too late, aren't we?"

Then I recognize the girl and in the same second she recognizes me and my heart freezes because she's about to say something and I can't let her.

"Hey, Cyrus!"

It's Ruth. From the Humane Society 7.

"This is my mom." She points to the woman and smiles. "Cyrus and I know each other from—"

"School!" I blurt. "From school. Ruth is in eighth grade, but she helped me find Mr. Hewett's class on the first day."

Ruth looks at me funny but then gives me a little half smile like she gets that something is up and she's on my team. "I had Mr. Hewett when I was in sixth grade," she says.

"Well, that was nice of you," my dad says. "I'm Brooks Olson. Cy's dad." He shakes their hands. "And you're a little late, but we can squeeze you in."

"No pun intended!" a nurse calls out and holds up a blue squeezy ball and a long needle still in its package.

"Don't look, Leo!" Sam says and gives him a friendly nudge with her elbow.

Leo pulls his arm away fast. "I told you—I just didn't have lunch."

The nurses get Ruth's mom set up in a chair and Ruth looks at me and nods toward the kitchen. I follow her, and in between bites of bagel and apple slices and in soft whispers that hide beneath her mom chatting and laughing with my dad and Sam, I tell her that my dad doesn't know about the humane society. That I'm surprising him by doing all this community service. The lie feels just as bad as all the others, because Ruth smiles and says, "I bet he'll be so proud of you. He seems really cool."

And that makes me think how lucky I am that I landed on the firehouse steps because the world is so big and I could have been left anywhere, but Brooks is my dad. And right where I belong.

"When are you going to tell him?" Ruth asks.

I look out at my dad, a Band-Aid pressed into the crook of his arm, thanking the nurses for coming today.

"I don't know," I say.

Her mom calls for her, and Ruth whispers that she'll see me later, like my secret is good with her.

Dad and I wait for the nurses to pack up the last station before we head to the car. I scan the radio past all the commercials and talking until I hear a song with a horn blasting and I turn it up.

Dad crumples a piece of paper and sticks it in the console, but it starts to unfold and I can read part of it. *Understanding Your Blood Type*, it says, and beneath, *Type O Negative* is circled. Dad is type O, just like Great-Grandpa Olson. I rub my fingers over the grooves of the dog tags beneath my sweatshirt and wonder, if it's not fighting fires or running passes into the end zone, what's in my blood?

CHAPTER 16

Mislabeled

Alejandro's locker is right across the hall from ours, and when he opens it, I can see the inside of the door is covered with pencil drawings held up with magnets. I have to get a little closer to see what the drawings are, so I kind of fake that I drop my calculator in the middle of the hall and sneak a peek. They're detailed dragons and castles and dark skies with bright moons and tall cities. They look professional, like the pages of a coloring book.

I pick up my calculator and put it in my book bag.

"He's good," Eduardo says and points to Alejandro's locker.

Alejandro smiles and shrugs his wide shoulders. "I just like drawing." And I can't believe he's using all that height and width and muscle to push a pencil along a page, and I wonder what Coach Matthews would say if he saw him.

I look at his drawings again. "Yeah," I say. "Really good. Do you play any sports?"

Alejandro puts a sketchbook in his bag, closes his locker, and laughs a little. "No way," he says. "I'm definitely more art room than locker room."

He says it so easily, like he's known right where he belongs for a long time, like Sam and her sisters, and it reminds me of what Sam said. *As long as you love it.* I wish I could say something that easily too. Just hand Coach my eighty-eight jersey and say, nope, all this sweating and smashing is not for me. That even though I'm not sure exactly where I belong, I know it's not on any yard line.

Alejandro and Eduardo say a few quick words in Spanish, then Eduardo reaches way up and Alejandro meets his hand for a high five, and I still can't believe they're twins. Alejandro walks in long strides toward Ms. Freeman's homeroom, and I wonder if kids in there look at him out of the corners of their eyes like they look at Eduardo in our classroom, or if they laugh behind their hands, or behind his back.

Or maybe that's just in our class, because we have Marcus and Shane, and everyone else just follows along. Even me, kind of.

Ms. Freeman says good morning to Alejandro. He disappears into the classroom, and Eduardo and I walk into Mr. Hewett's room.

My face flushes hot because I'm sure everyone remembers what happened yesterday, how I ran down the hall to the bathroom and came back with watery cry eyes even though I tried my best to blink all the tears out before opening the door.

And then I hear Marcus whisper to Shane, "It's Cyrus and Sissy."

I want to say something, like how Sam told Leo to use his big-boy voice and say it out loud for everyone to hear if he's so tough and brave. I open my mouth, but their laughter fades out and I miss my chance and my throat is starting to feel all scratchy and closed. And I hate that I can't get my tongue to work quick enough.

Eduardo sits down at his table with Joel and Benji, and I take one more step toward my table in the back but I stop. And inside I say a great big, loud *NO*. And even though I only say it inside, it shouts to the tips of my fingers and toes and it clamps my teeth down hard. *NO*. I step back and pull out the extra chair at Eduardo's table. "Can I sit here instead?"

Eduardo smiles and nods, and Marcus huffs a loud snort out of his nose and mumbles, "Maybe it's Sissy and Sissy."

That's the first time Marcus has ever called me a name in the six years I've known him, and it knocks the wind out of me like a helmet to the gut.

Mr. Hewett tells us that he's going to give us time in class to work on our book reviews after today's read-aloud, then he calls us over to the rug area. We've already given up grumbling about Mr. Hewett's picture books because I'm pretty sure it's everyone's favorite part of the whole day, when he reads to us and we can just sit on the rug like little kids and talk about stories. I'm just glad that today he's doing the reading so I can listen and think and follow the pictures.

I try not to look at Marcus and Shane when they sit in the back; instead I glance up at Mr. Hewett's bulletin board. The cover of *Oliver Button Is a Sissy* is hanging next to *Ish* and *Calvin Can't Fly*, and because I'm good at math I quickly count down and across the grid to see how many squares are for picture-book covers. There are 180 total, and I think that's some kind of record. Reading 180 books in one school year.

Even though I'm trying to look everywhere else, I see Zander joining Marcus and Shane in the back, and they're all laughing about something and I wonder if it's me. And that makes my cheeks burn hot and my heart thump harder and achier than when I'm in touch-and-goes, and it makes me wish I could shrink smaller than four feet eight inches.

I sit next to Eduardo near the front, and I hear someone whispering, "Are they like friends now?" That makes my cheeks burn even hotter, so I face forward toward Mr. Hewett and the picture book he's holding up because I don't really want anyone to think Eduardo and I are friends, but I also actually kind of think he's nice, and both those feelings are smashing headfirst into each other right below my great-grandpa Olson's dog tags.

The book today is about a blue crayon in a red wrapper, and even though it feels silly that we're in sixth grade and reading a story about a crayon, everyone is leaning forward and raising their hands and pointing to the pages. All the other crayons in the book are trying to figure out what is wrong with Red. They try all sorts of things to fix him, but nothing changes: he is who he is, and everything comes out blue. At the end of the book, the rest of the crayons understand there's nothing wrong with him at all, he's just not red. He's blue. He was just mislabeled, and even though his strawberries are off and he can't mix to make orange, he can draw the most perfect ocean.

Mr. Hewett invites us to turn and talk to our partner, and before I can look to my right and team up with Nora, Eduardo turns to me and says, "I can't believe crayons do this too!"

Nora scoots around the other way, to Emily, and everyone else is teaming up and starting to talk.

Eduardo keeps going. "I mean, I get that *we* do it all the time because it's hard to look at someone and see what they're like on their insides. But come on, crayons! 'Red' had blue sticking out everywhere! Open your crayon-eyes!" He makes quotation marks in the air with his fingers when he says *Red* and splats his palm to his forehead when he finishes. That makes me laugh, and I forget to try to hide it in my shirtsleeve.

I wasn't thinking of the story like that, and now I like it even more and kind of wish Mr. Hewett would read it all over again.

"Yeah," I say. "Everyone just expected him to draw strawberries, but he's not a strawberry drawer! He's an ocean drawer!" It feels like something opens up wide in me, like when I read along with Grandma's *na na na*s, like when Mr. Fletcher picked up the trombone and slid the notes down the slide and back up again. I get a little too excited and I say it a little too loud and I don't even care that Marcus is probably snickering in the back and Shane is probably following right along.

Eduardo sticks his hand out for a high five, and even though high fives are dorky and fist bumps are cooler, I give him five and it feels good, our palms meeting and making a perfect clap.

Mr. Hewett tells us it's work time and he'll come around to our tables as we get started on our book reviews.

Eduardo and I go back to our table, and he asks me which book I chose to write about.

"*Wonder.*" I pull it out of my bag, and I'm hoping he doesn't ask me any questions because I'm only on page sixteen.

"I love that book!"

I don't mean to tell him this because my plan is to fake finish, watch the movie, and write the review before it's due, but my throat does the opposite of closing up around him and the words just fall out of my mouth. "I haven't actually finished it, but I still know it's the best book I've ever read."

All he says is, "I won't ruin the ending, then." I don't tell him I'm nowhere near the end.

Then he goes up to Mr. Hewett's chalkboard tray and asks if he can borrow *Oliver Button Is a Sissy* again.

When he comes back to our table, he takes out his printed copy with all the little notes from yesterday. Then he opens to each page of Mr. Hewett's book, studying the pictures and adding to his jots. Zander walks by our table and says, "Wait, are you writing your review on that?"

Eduardo doesn't even look up. He just nods his head

and jots another idea. "Yup. I've read lots of books," he says, eyes still on the pictures. "But this one is the best." He flips another page.

Zander snorts, and I watch him roll his eyes toward my old table. Then he says, "The kid with the Velcro shoes is writing about the sissy picture book." Marcus and Shane laugh and I can't believe they are my friends from forever and I'm starting to hear that big *NO* inside me again but Mr. Hewett is at the table next to them and he's quicker. He tells Zander and Marcus and Shane to get up *right now* and he sounds serious and they all shuffle out of the classroom behind him.

"Oooooooh, they're in trouble," Nora sings.

I want to hear what Mr. Hewett is saying to them out there. I don't hear yelling, so I wonder if he's like my dad, who has a quiet way of making you understand exactly what you did wrong and how terrible it was.

I try to read a page of *Wonder* with *one-and-two-and-three-and-four-and* in my head and swaying a little to each sentence without making it obvious, and my brain is following right along OK and I can't believe how mean Julian is being to Auggie when he tours the new school. He makes fun of the way Auggie looks and assumes he isn't smart and I want to jump right in the book and tell him NO. Tell him to stop.

Marcus opens the classroom door and Shane, Zander,

and Mr. Hewett follow him back in. The smirk on Marcus's face tells me that whatever talk they got out there didn't work. As soon as they sit back down, he makes a gesture like he's pulling up a Velcro strap and makes the sound, *shick-shick*. They laugh silent little laughs and Mr. Hewett doesn't hear them, or at least he fakes that he doesn't, because he sits at another table group and asks them what they're working on and leans over their pages to see their writing.

I keep reading *Wonder*, but I'm going too fast now and my brain wanders and thinks of every little thing other than the book—Parker's wagging tail, and the fake I have planned to get out of practice today, Defeat of Jesse James Days and how instead of sitting on top of the truck and watching the parade I have to sit on the bench in my uniform and watch the A Team, and how Marcus and Shane will probably laugh at me, and the band permission slip sticking out of Eduardo's notebook, and September ninth.

And by the time the bell rings for next period, I've turned four pages and I don't know what happened to Auggie at all, but I bet Julian hasn't gotten any nicer, just like Marcus and Shane, and just like Leo, and I'm wondering why everyone is so obsessed with labels.

CHAPTER 17

NO

The band has their first practice after school today. Eduardo waves bye and heads down the hall and I forgot to ask what instrument he circled on the back of the form and I want to stand up and follow all the kids walking to band to find out who circled the trombone and gets to practice letting the slide rise and fall today.

At least today is Friday, a Parker day.

My last Parker day.

In the locker room, I pretend I'm washing my hands, but I rub a little soap in my eyes until they're red so when I tell Coach Matthews that I think I have pink eye I have something to point to.

On the field I trot over to him and blink hard and say it burns and ask if I can go call my dad from the office. I'm expecting him to wave me off because usually when you say *pink eye*, people back up two steps. But Coach Matthews pulls me in by the face mask and looks right into my eyes.

"Nope," he says. "I know pink eye, and that's not it. You probably just have something stuck in there. Blink lots and try not to rub them." Then he pats my shoulder and nudges me toward Assistant Coach Erikson at the far end of the field in a way that says *Now get back out there*. But I don't want to get back out there.

Marcus and Shane have stopped tossing the ball and are watching me. I'm thinking maybe they feel sorry that they called me *Sissy* and they're going to quit being mean and we can all just go back to being friends again and talk about the Vikings and toss footballs in our backyards and give Heywood Hurrahs and fist bumps all season. Because that would be easier than not sitting with them in class and wondering why they're acting the way they're acting, and if they're laughing at me. And maybe if I just trot to Assistant Coach Erikson and work hard and catch balls I can move up to the A Team and we can have everything back to just how it was.

But there's something louder in me. That big, huge *NO* that's forcing its way up from my gut.

And I don't care if Coach Matthews believes my pink eye or not because I don't want to trot out there, not one tiny bit, and today is September sixth, and that means no more Tuesdays or Fridays before they take Parker away, so it's today or never again.

And before I know it, I'm yelling it across the field.

"NO!"

A few players look over, their jaws hanging open with orange mouth guards floating above their tongues. Marcus holds his arms out like *No what?*

"Come on, Olson!" Assistant Coach Erikson calls from the far side of the field, where the B Team is lacing up their cleats.

But I can almost feel Parker's nose on my left shoulder, and I blink a hundred times fast so my tears don't slide out.

"NO!"

"Olson," Coach Matthews says, then juts his chin toward the field. Both teams are coming together in a circle for stretches, and it's a circle I know I don't want to be in.

"No."

I take off my helmet and the cool air on my head feels good and right and I know more than anything that I need to get off this field and to Parker fast before volunteer walking hours are over, but I don't have another fake planned and all I can say is, "No."

"No what, Olson?" Coach says.

He's looking down at me and tapping his clipboard against his palm.

"No football."

I walk toward the sideline bench to pick up my bag. "Sorry," I say, and I hate that I say that because I'm not really sorry. I'm more sorry that I said sorry.

"Olson, you can't just leave. If you walk off the field, you won't sit with us tomorrow. You'll be off the B Team and won't get the training you need for next year." He puts his whistle in his mouth. "And I don't think that's what you want," he says. A little whistle escapes around his words.

He's wrong. That's exactly what I want. So before I can chicken out, I hand him my helmet, and my sticky wide receiver gloves, and pull my jersey eighty-eight over my head.

I unlace my pinchy cleats, and I don't know what to do with them because if I take them with me there's a chance they'll end up back on my feet, so I leave them on the bench for some other kid who will fit in them perfectly. I slide on my Vans, wave to Marcus and Shane, who are shaking their heads in their big helmets, and run right off the field and down the sidewalk, away from Joseph Lee Heywood Middle School.

I don't know what I'll do when Coach Matthews calls my dad. All I know is that it's Friday. It's a Parker day.

When I get there I see Lou, Ruth, Elli, and DeeDee outside the humane society.

"Closed," Lou says.

"What do you mean 'closed'?" I ask. "It's Friday."

DeeDee looks at me with sad eyes. "The vet just got here for vaccines."

But that *NO* is still rattling around in me, and I don't even know how my hand gets balled into a fist and how it starts pounding on the door until Max from the front desk opens it up and I fall in and say, "It's Friday."

"I know, Cyrus, but—"

I don't stay to hear the rest of what Max has to say. Instead I rush down the hall and knock on the doors that swing into the back, where I can hear the dogs yipping and panting.

A woman in green hospital scrubs comes out. "Can I help you?"

"I'm here to walk Parker." I try to look past her into the back room.

She lifts the mask off her mouth and rests it on top of her head. "Are you his owner?"

I feel the *NO* that's banging around inside me fall and curl up right there in my gut.

Max is coming down the hall quickly. "Cyrus," she says. "Parker is getting his shots today while the veterinarian is here." She looks at me and puts her hand on my shoulder, and it feels like I wait a hundred minutes until she says, "I'm sorry."

"But this is a Parker day," I say. "It's the last Parker day."

The rest of The 7 is here now, and June is asking what's going on and Katherine and Alexis are peeking down the hallway trying to see the dogs.

Katherine steps in and asks, "Can't he say goodbye at least?"

Max looks at the veterinarian and the veterinarian nods her head OK and turns back through the double doors.

As soon as I hear Parker's nails clicking across the floor, I crouch down, and by the time he sees me and trots through the hall my tears are splashing big splats on the floor between my toe-dragged shoes, and even though my shoulders are shaking, Parker parks his nose right there under my ear and I hold on tight.

DeeDee rubs little circles on my back as I hug him, and it feels good but makes me cry harder and Alexis says she's so sorry and that Parker deserves someone like me, and that makes me think about how when I'm with Parker I feel like I'm right where I belong. That he's what my grandma calls a happy place.

I kiss Parker's face and that *NO* wakes back up. "No,"

I say. "He doesn't deserve someone *like* me. He deserves *me*." Because everyone should have a shoulder they can lay their head on.

I want to get to my dad before Coach Matthews does, so I run. And The 7 runs with me—even DeeDee, who's wearing thin, flat shoes that flap against the pavement. And between panting breaths, I tell them everything about how my dad said no to Parker and no to walking him and no to even naming him. I tell them that I've been faking. Faking a lot. And I'm done with faking. I tell them how I quit football even though I'm an Olson and that I have to tell my dad that I'm not a wide receiver and that Parker needs us right now.

The smokestacks just outside of town pump out big clouds and the air smells like Cheerios baking, and it smells like home, and for some reason it's making me feel like maybe everything is going to be OK.

When we reach the center of town, we slow down a little and dodge people walking on the sidewalk, but we don't stop until we get to the firehouse parking lot.

When I put my hand on the knob, I wonder, like I always do, if I'm stepping right on the spot where I was left in my tight-swaddled baby blanket, crying into the night. The very spot where Parker whimpered for me.

The big door is heavy, and when I pull it open I can

feel The 7 behind me and hear their breath, still quick and shallow from the run.

The door flies open fast, and I almost fall backward because my dad is pushing it out at the same time. He's moving so quick that he runs straight into me and my face smushes right into his firefighter's T-shirt and the rough canvas of his suspender strap. His hands grip my biceps, his fingers fitting all the way around, and it feels, at first, like he wants to squeeze my twiggy little arms and shake me hard because I lied and lied and lied, but then it feels more like a hug, an all-the-way-around hug like Grandma used to give, and I don't even know what he knows yet, except I know that whatever it is, it'll be OK.

Then he's kneeling down and letting me rest my head right there on his big shoulder, the strap of his suspender beneath my cheek. "Cyrus," he whispers. "Cyrus, Cyrus, Cyrus. You scared me again."

He must see The 7 behind me because he asks, "Who are your friends?" And I'm glad that's the first question he asks me, because I know all the others are going to be *Why did you lie?* and *What happened at practice?* and *Where were you?*

June steps forward and reaches out her hand. "We're the Humane Society 7." Then she looks at me. "But really I guess we're more like The 8 now." And my heart feels like it explodes with happy, foot-tapping jazz music because their circle feels like one of Grandma's all-the-way-around hugs too.

Dad raises his eyebrows at me when June says *Humane Society*. He stands up and shakes her hand and then everyone else's.

Then he looks down at me, and he's not even asking any questions because he doesn't have to. He's waiting for me to do all the explaining. And even though I ran here to tell him about Parker and how he has to reconsider his no-pet policy and that we have to adopt him fast or I won't get to see him anymore, not even on Tuesdays and Fridays, not ever, my throat is all scratchy and closing up and I just stare down at my unlaced Vans.

"Coach Matthews called," he says.

I look up and right into Dad's worried eyes and try to tell him that I had to leave football practice and that we have to save Parker from moving to another humane society, where no one will know him and no one will visit him, and even if his real owner couldn't take care of him, I can and I want to.

I open my mouth, but then I hear Leo slide down the pole and land on his feet. Sam follows behind him.

"Cy!" he bellows. "What's this I hear about you quitting football? Olsons aren't quitters. Right, Brooks?" He claps my dad on the shoulder.

Dad pulls his shoulder away.

"I'm sorr—" I start, but then I hear Katherine's voice, quiet but steady, behind me.

"You're not a quitter, Cy."

And I feel that *NO* rise up in me again. And I'm not sorry. I'm not sorry I quit football because I didn't quit Parker.

I look at Sam, and she gives me a little nod like it's time to use my big-boy voice and so I do. I clear my throat and say it right out loud.

"I'm not sorry."

Dad just waits, like he always does, for the whole story. "Start at the beginning, Cy."

And with The 7 behind me, and Sam nodding me on, I say, "I don't like playing football."

I almost tell him about how I think I might be mislabeled. That I don't have that Olson gene. I'm not a wide receiver or a war hero and I don't want to fight fires or ever do another touch-and-go in my whole life. That I like picture books and tapping my foot and I think the trombone might be the best sound in the whole world. And I want Parker to live with us because holding his head on my shoulder is right where I belong.

And for one second I think I might tell him about Mr. Hewett's book *Red*, but it's not as good without the pictures and I can't remember the whole way it goes, so instead I say, "I didn't want to make any team. I haven't liked football since we stopped two-hand touch."

His shoulders sink an inch, and I think mine do too because I hate upsetting him.

But I can't stop now, not with Parker getting his shots and leaving the humane society.

So I keep telling and telling him the whole story with no fakes at all. "And I'm not sure Marcus and Shane are nice either. I know they're really good at football and I've known them forever, but there's a new kid in our class and they call him *Edweirdo*."

Leo chuckles and I look up at him and raise my shoulders back up that inch, and I bark that *NO* right out. "That's NOT funny!"

That makes Leo stop laughing fast. Sam smiles and gives me a little thumbs-up and nods for me to keep on, so I look back at Dad and say, "And I've been visiting Parker."

Deep creases wrinkle across his forehead, and I know what he's saying. He's saying that seeing Parker will only make it harder.

"And on Monday they're transferring him to another humane society an hour from here and . . ." I try to say *and he won't have my shoulder and I won't have his and*

I know you said no but I think we should adopt him anyway, but I think if I keep talking I'll start crying, so I stop.

Now it's my turn to wait and watch as Dad rubs the folds on his forehead and sighs deep out of his nose.

"I wish you'd told me" is all he says. Then he takes a big breath and adds, "About all of it."

And even if I could think of what to say next, and say it without crying, I would be cut off by the static blast on Dad's radio. Long strings of numbers and letters and codes and things I don't understand crackle through, and Dad holds up his finger—*shhhh*—and presses his ear toward his radio.

Sam moves fast, opening the big garage doors and calling out the engine numbers. Dad shoos The 7 out the door. They all move quick and shout, "Bye," as the big door slams behind them. Then he sounds the alarm and I hear it scream through Northfield, sing down Division Street, and echo off the brick buildings.

I know the plan. The plan is that I throw my bag back over my shoulders, push open the big door, step over the spot where I was left eleven years ago, walk to Grandma's apartment, and wait with her until we hear from Dad. But as soon as I step outside, I hear the static voice on the radio.

"212 Third Street."

I know where that is because the humane society is 210 Third Street. And the voice crackles and spits and they sound the alarm again and I know this isn't just a cat up a tree or a contained trash can flame from a scared kid. And I know what my dad says about fires. They spread fast.

The siren wails, warning the town and calling the EMTs and volunteers to help, and my dad calls out, "Go to Grandma's!" and presses on the gas of the fire engine and whizzes past me, lights flashing.

I rub my great-grandpa Olson's dog tags beneath my shirt and think about rubbing Parker's fur behind his ears, and for the third time today, I run. I run right away from the plan and in the opposite direction of Grandma's apartment, and I do what Dad told me never to do. I run right toward the fire.

CHAPTER 18

Flames

Even from blocks away, I can see smoke clouding above the buildings and clogging the air, turning the smell of baking Cheerios into soot. I can feel it scratch at my lungs.

Dad pulls the fire truck over and stops right in front of the pizza shop. The lights flash red and blue, and the black smoke rises higher and higher in the sky.

I keep running and running, coughing into my sleeve, my eyes burning, and when I get closer I see loud orange flames punch through the side window of the shop with a *pop!* Glass shatters, and the force of the fire spits little shards across the ground, toward the humane society. The flames blast brighter and hotter, reaching.

The fire is big and angry and growing.

My legs stop running.

Half a block away, I slip behind a tree and watch.

Chief Reynolds is there and everyone's moving fast, shouting demands. Passersby stop to watch, and my Dad yells for them to keep moving as he tries to organize the volunteer firefighters who are rushing toward the truck to set up cones and direct traffic, and I can't take my eyes off the stretching flames.

It feels like night already because the smoke is filling the sky and smothering the sun and I have to squint to see all the workers moving fast.

I know exactly what they're all doing too, because I've heard it a hundred times in their trainings at the firehouse. They're assessing the fire and finding a good entry point. Then they have two things to do right away: One, find any victims. Two, locate the source of the fire and make a plan to snuff it out.

The flames are spilling fast out of the pizza shop window and licking long tongues toward the humane society, and I want to sprint and push through the front door and get all the dogs out of their crates and let them run after me down the hall and outside and across the street where they're safe and get down on my knees so Parker can find my shoulder easy.

But the more the fire pours from the side window, the more my feet feel like they're stuck in ice.

I'm frozen.

And I can't thaw out. I can't make a move toward the humane society, toward Parker, toward the fire.

Then I see my dad. He's facing away from the fire, taking in a big breath. I know because even from here I can see his big shoulders rise up. And then he straps on his mask, turns, and rushes right through the front door of the pizza shop.

Leo is pulling a hose from the truck, and Sam takes that same big breath that lifts up her shoulders and disappears fast right through the front door of the humane society.

I try to run after her so I can tell her where they keep the leashes and how Parker doesn't like if you pull him by the collar, but my feet won't move, and I can't take my eyes from the front door of the pizza shop.

Because I'm watching for the door to fly back open.

I'm watching for Dad. Like when a player goes down on the field and all you can do is take a knee and wait and wait for them to get up and be OK while your heart beats loud in your ears and you can hear your own blood *swoosh*ing around and echoing off your helmet.

The red and blue lights keep flashing across the

front of the pizza shop, right over the door, and without even trying I can hear my grandma's *one-and-two-and-three-and-four-and*, so I count along with it—*one-and-two-and-three-and-four-and-one-and-two-and-three-and-four-and*. The rhythm slows down the pounding in my ears and I try to take in those deep breaths that lift my shoulders up, but even from here I can smell the smoke and it makes me cough.

One-and-two-and-three-and-four-and. I know it's only been sixteen seconds, but it feels like minutes.

One-and-two-and-three-and—then the door flies back open and Dad comes out. He gives quick all-clear signals to Leo and two volunteers at the truck. Then Sam rushes back out of the humane society with Max and the veterinarian and a herd of dogs wiggling and wagging and sending their yips and barks into the smoke-choked air.

I peek around the tree and squint my eyes and there's Parker, panting and yipping.

I almost get my feet unstuck when there's a loud *pop!* and *snap!* And something falls and the dogs bark and Max's trying to clip them all into their leashes and Sam is opening her arms wide and herding them all down the sidewalk away from the fire, and Leo and a volunteer start unrolling yellow caution tape that tells me to stay back, turn around, hurry away. So I do.

I turn around and run. And the whole way I'm thinking, I'm not brave like that. Brave like put-out-a-fire brave. Brave like break-through-the-caution-tape brave. Brave like my dad.

CHAPTER 19

One-and-Two-and-Three-and-Four-and

When I get to Grandma's building, there's a tall man with a mustache sitting at the piano in the lobby, and even though my heart is still racing fast away from the fire, as soon as I hear the music, my feet slow and I walk on the beat of the notes to where Grandma is sitting with her eyes closed.

I sit down at her left side, and she doesn't have to open her eyes to know it's me. She pats my knee with her good hand and says, "Na na na." And I know what she's saying, because I know my grandma. She's telling me to close my eyes too. Firehouse emergency days are hard for both of us. And I think Grandma's hand needs my knee as much as my knee needs her hand.

"Na na?" she asks.

"A fire," I say, and her hand squeezes my knee a little harder because we both always wish it were just a cat up a tree.

"Na na na," she tells me again.

I don't really want to close my eyes because we're not the only ones sitting here listening and I'm pretty sure I'll look funny doing it, but I close them anyway because Grandma looks relaxed and the music sounds good and I'm wondering if maybe the older you get the less you care if others think you look funny or not.

I'm glad I close my eyes with Grandma because it helps me hear only the notes of the piano. My brain is trying to pull me back to the *pop*s and *crack*s of the fire. And wondering if my dad has run back through that door yet, and if he found the source of the fire, and if he could act fast before it spread to the humane society. And where they brought Parker. And if they took my T-shirt from his kennel before they ran out.

The piano music gets higher and lower, and I focus my brain on imagining the man's hands flying up the keys and back down. It makes me think of Mr. Fletcher dropping the trombone slide and pulling it back up. And I know there are lots of people sitting around and listening and closing their eyes and swaying to the music, but it feels like the notes are talking right to me and they're saying *Shhhh, it's OK*.

Then the notes and chords start to sound familiar, and the man at the piano is turning this song into another one, one I know. "Somewhere Over the Rainbow." Grandma takes her hand from my knee, and I open my eyes to see her pat the spot right over her heart. Then she sings. "Na naaaa na na na na naa." Her voice rises and dips and I whisper to her, "Dad used to sing this song to me."

She opens her eyes and nudges me with her elbow and smiles. Then she points to herself and says, "Na na na na na na!" And I know what she's saying. She's telling me that this is *her* song and who do I think sang it to my dad before he sang it to me? I smile and she closes her eyes again. She sings along with the pianist and I can feel the music from my ears all the way down through my heart and out my tapping feet.

I try to picture Grandma sitting on the edge of my dad's bed just like he used to sit on mine when I couldn't sleep, singing about troubles melting like lemon drops. But all I can picture is my dad in his uniform, number eighty-eight, fielding passes with sticky-palmed gloves that never fumble and running straight on toward the end zone. Or in his suspenders and big boots and firefighter's jacket running headfirst into the fire. I close my eyes again and listen to the music, and little by little I can. I can imagine him tucked in tight, his heart beat calming with each note, Grandma squeezing his hand in hers, giving him strength. And I wonder if maybe people who are brave like that, brave like barrel-into-a-defensive-back brave, are also scared sometimes too.

When the song ends, Milly comes to help my grandma back to her room. "Anita," she says, and I can tell she's being playful because she throws out a hip and cocks her head to the side. "Where is your cane?"

Grandma says, "Na na na," and waves her off. And I know she's saying *Oh, you forget that right now. I don't need any cane.*

When she first had her stroke, the doctor said she'd never walk on her own again. She looked right at him, raised her left hand from beneath her hospital sheet, pointed her finger at the *Dr. Cole* stitched on his coat, and said one clear, loud "Na." Now every day she gets up on her own two feet to show how wrong he was.

The doctor also said she'd never be able to talk again. That part turned out to be true. But I think my grandma found out there's more than one way to say what you mean.

Milly walks half a step behind us just in case, all the way to Grandma's apartment door, and helps her into her chair. Then she winks at me and says, "I'll go see what I can find for you in the kitchen."

Grandma runs her fingers over the remote, but she doesn't turn on the TV, because we don't watch TV on firehouse emergency nights anymore, even if the Vikings are playing or the Twins are in the playoffs. On our first fire emergency sleepover, we turned on the TV to find the Twins game. But now we know we can't flick through all the breaking local news, the lights flashing, and reporters gathering. We just sit and wait, and try to keep our brains on something else, until we hear from Dad.

I run my finger along Grandma's records and stop on Marvin Gaye, *What's Going On*. Grandma puts her hand over her heart and closes her eyes and I drop the needle in the groove and Marvin Gaye starts singing about how there's too many of us crying and the song sings right into my heart because it makes tears burn behind my eyes and I don't even care when one leaks down my cheek.

I think the music is singing right to Grandma's heart too, because she sighs deep and changes the subject.

"Na na na na na!" she says and pulls her arm back like she's throwing a football long, but football is the last thing I want to talk about.

For one second, I think maybe I'll fake like I can't figure out what she's talking about, but that feels worse than the truth, and Grandma always has a way of pulling out what's way down deep in me anyway. So I inhale and let the breath raise up my shoulders. Then I tell her.

"I quit football, Grandma."

"Na!" she says. Just one clear *na!* as definite as the *na!* she told Dr. Cole in the hospital when he said she'd never walk again. But the way she's looking at me, with the left side of her face curling up, trying at a smile, makes me think that she isn't saying *No!*—I think she might be saying *Good!* or *Finally!*

"I'm just not brave like that."

She raises an eyebrow and curls her hand at me like *Tell me more.* So I do. I tell her about Marcus and Shane and how they're really good—good like Dad was good. And how they like going to practice and running routes and sending balls long and slamming into big defenders and coming out of a pig pile with the ball. And how they spit through their face masks and laugh at a boy named Eduardo because he's different.

This makes the creases in Grandma's forehead cut deeper.

"Na." And this time I'm sure that she's saying *No.*

And I don't know why exactly, but I start telling Grandma more about Eduardo. "He's new and he's small and he wears Velcro shoes and he's doing his first English project on a picture book."

"Na na?" she says and puts her left fist on her hip.

So what? she asked, except it sounded more like a statement than a question. And I'm thinking, *So what?* is right. *So what?* is exactly right.

I shrug my shoulders.

She starts using her left hand to gesture again. "Na na na na na na na na na na na." She's jumping from one thing to the next and I'm trying to follow. "Na na na! Na na?" I know she's upset about Marcus and Shane being mean, but I don't know exactly what she's saying or how to respond. I sort of feel like I should say I'm sorry. I'm sorry that I couldn't look Marcus and Shane and everyone else who just followed along right in the eye and say, *So what?*

Then Grandma's gesturing again, a football behind her head, then holding her palm up to the ceiling like she's saying *Why?* or *How?*

"It was OK when it was two-hand touch in Mighty-Mites. After that I only really played because Dad did, and because Marcus and Shane did. Quitting wasn't so hard," I tell her. "Especially because of Parker."

Saying his name makes my heart jump because it makes me think of the fire again and I hope he's OK and not scared and that they took him somewhere warm. And it makes me think of Dad and whether he's found the source yet and snuffed it out.

I tell Grandma about Parker, how he was all alone and skinny and shivering when he showed up at the firehouse and Dad said no. I tell her all about the humane society and The 7 and how Parker's more important to me than football or Marcus or Shane.

Grandma sits back in her chair. She's thinking about everything I just told her, and all that quiet makes me think about it too. And mostly I'm thinking that I hope I didn't make Dad disappointed. Disappointed that I snuck behind his back. That I'm not a wide receiver.

It just stays like that, quiet, for thinking, until Milly comes in with two chocolate cupcakes on a paper plate. "Found a little something for you," she says and puts them down on the coffee table.

I love dessert-before-dinner days. It's kind of my grandma's and my thing, and we never tell my dad, which is also going behind his back but doesn't feel as bad because it's only cake. Before Grandma's stroke, she used to slide a plate of homemade cookies across the table at five o'clock and say, "Live a little." Then, with a full, laughing mouth, she'd say, "Our secret."

"These were baked this morning," Milly tells us. "I *might* have tasted the frosting while they were decorating, just to make sure they were good enough for our residents. It's a hard job, but somebody has to do it." She sighs big and shrugs.

That makes me laugh, and the laugh makes my shoulders sink down like I just dropped the weight of too-big pads from my frame. "Thanks," I say.

She smiles. *"De nada."*

I've heard Milly say *de nada* and *gracias* and call my grandma Anita Bonita a hundred times, but it isn't until right this second that I realize those are Spanish words, and that makes me feel really slow, but I don't really hear a lot of other languages and at Joseph Lee Heywood Middle School you don't pick between Spanish or French class until seventh grade.

"Milly," I say. She stops at the door. "Do you speak Spanish?"

"Sí, claro," she responds. I can tell that means yes. I'm not that slow. And I tell her that my friend at school does too and that next year when we get to choose, I'm going to pick Spanish. "My name is Milagros," she tells me. "It means *miracle*." Then she winks and closes the door.

Miracle is exactly right, I'm thinking. I can't imagine this place without Milly.

Grandma grips the arm of her chair and tries to scoot to the edge, but I can see it's hard for her to get momentum, so I hold behind her elbow like I've seen Dad do and help her move forward. I don't make a big deal about it because Grandma doesn't like anyone fussing over her.

I sit back down on the couch, and she leans forward and pushes the plate of cupcakes toward me. "Na na na," she says. *It's our little secret.*

We both take bites and laugh and wish that we could take our minds more off Dad and the fire. It's dark outside now and Marvin Gaye is singing about *oh, mercy mercy me* and Grandma gestures to my book bag. She might spoil me with dessert before dinner, but she also always makes sure I do all my homework. "You'll thank me someday," she used to say. And when I'd finish, she'd read to me way past my bedtime.

I do my math problems while Grandma peeks over at my graph paper notebook. I quickly cross out numbers and subtract things from each side of the equation, then divide and find X. It's six. That was an easy one, but Grandma still says, "Na na!" and puts her arm out like she has no idea how I did that so fast.

"You just have to get X by itself," I tell her.

Milly comes back in with a menu for dinner. I look down at it and only read the main course written in big letters for all the old people to read. I already know that if I start trying to read about all the sides and sauces, I won't remember what the choices are and end up pointing to something called meat loaf, and I know I don't want that again.

Grandma points to the first choice. Haddock. I look

up at her and she says, "Na," and tries to make a fish face and turn her left hand into a flapping fin. Milly and I laugh, and I point to the second one, ravioli.

"One haddock and one ravioli coming right up," Milly says, and leaves again for the kitchen.

I tell Grandma I don't have any other homework even though I do. What I didn't realize would be so hard about middle school is that we change classrooms and teachers for every subject and it doesn't seem like it all goes together. The hardest part is that each class has reading. A lot of reading. So the rest of my homework is printed copies of textbook pages, and I don't think I can relax my brain enough to slow down and find the rhythm and think between each sentence like Grandma taught me. Not with Dad fighting a fire and Parker being herded down the street and away.

She raises her eyebrows like she doesn't believe that's all the homework I have, and I want to tell her that it's Friday, so I don't have to do it all right now anyway. Then she folds her hand into the shape of a book and pretends to read her palm. "Na na na?"

I don't want to tell her that I've only read eight more pages of *Wonder* and that for most of the pages I didn't slow down and find the rhythm and think after each sentence, so I don't know exactly what Auggie is doing right now, which makes it even harder to open the book back up.

"I left it at school," I tell her, and before the fake feels too bad in my gut, Milly comes in with dinner. She folds out a tray for Grandma and helps her scoot to the edge of her chair.

"Na na na na na!" she says and points to her fish. It's already cut into bite-sized pieces and Grandma is saying *No, Milly. You don't have to do that.* But Milly just smiles and hustles out, and I'm thinking that was a good move because you can't just straight up help Grandma. You have to go at it sneaky like that.

After we eat, I take the cushions off the couch and pull out the bed. Neither one of says anything, but I know we're both trying to remember that fighting fires takes time and no news is good news and right now, other families need him.

Milly comes back to help Grandma in the bathroom and into her nightclothes. They close the door to her bedroom, but I can hear "Na na na," and I think she's saying a combination between *I can really do this on my own* and *Thank you*, because ever since her stroke my grandma's been taking naps during the day and getting tired earlier at night.

I lie down on the bed with my head propped up because I'm not ready for sleep yet. The door opens and Grandma points to the edge of my bed, so Milly helps her over. The bed sinks when she sits down and Milly says, "*Buenas noches*," and winks and closes the door.

Grandma smiles at me and sticks her left hand down into my book bag and pulls out *Wonder*. She looks at me like *Oh, here it is!* and opens it to the page I have dog-eared. She taps her shoulder, and I sit up next to her and put my head right there and help her hold the book open. Then she reads to me—"Na na na na na na"—and I follow the words along the page as she stops and sways after each sentence. I stop and think and sway too and follow Auggie through his first day of school.

I must have fallen asleep like that and Grandma must have pressed her pendant button for Milly to come help her to bed or maybe she clicked off the lamp and made her slow way herself, because when I wake up next it's Dad's suspender strap I feel on my cheek. At first I think it's a dream and I'm that tiny baby being rocked and rocked in the hospital, but it's really him. He's here and he's safe and he's lying down next to me and even though he's not wearing his uniform jacket anymore he still smells a little like smoke. But I don't care. I breathe through my mouth and keep my head right on his sus-pender strap anyway.

I want to ask him about Parker and if the fire spread and does he know where they took the dogs? But I don't want to remind him about sneaking behind his back and I don't want him to know that I followed the truck to the fire, then chickened out and ran away. So I just keep on pretending to sleep and try not to think about all the mess I'm in. How I walked off the field, away from Coach Matthews and toward Parker, and that I told my dad the whole thing.

Now I'm not sure what it'll be like at Defeat of Jesse James Days tomorrow. Whether I'll apologize to Coach Matthews and sit on the bench with my zero-zero or whether I'll watch from the top of the fire truck with the crew like I usually do. Or whether I'll be grounded and stuck in my room like I deserve.

I count my breaths in and out, one-and-two-and-three-and-four-and-one-and-two-and-three-and-four, and before I fall back asleep I feel Dad's breath warm near my ear.

"Parker is fine."

I don't want to give up that I'm fake sleeping, but I'm so excited that he's OK and that Dad used his name, Parker. I keep my eyes closed and wait a beat and then whisper back.

"Thanks."

CHAPTER 20

Reenactment

We wake up early in Grandma's apartment, and even from in here I can feel the buzz of the town. Defeat of Jesse James Days is the same as waking up on Christmas morning or on a snow day, when before you even open your eyes you just know that something is special.

Everyone in Northfield is waking up early too, packing their folding chairs, pouring their thermoses full of coffee, and getting ready to stake out a seat on the side of Division Street to wait for Jesse James and his gang to fly through town and attempt to rob our bank. It doesn't matter that we know the ending. Joseph Lee Heywood refuses to open the safe, and Northfield fires back and saves their bank. Every year it's just as exciting, and everyone sits on the edge of their folded chairs and leans in from the curb as if maybe this year there'll be a different outcome.

Dad quietly folds the bed back into the couch, and I put my math notebook and *Wonder* in my book bag. We're trying not to wake Grandma, so we're not talking, but I want to ask him about the fire and how it started and if the flames ever reached the humane society.

Grandma must hear us anyway, because she starts calling from her bedroom. There are loud creaks and grunts and I imagine her trying to sit up and I think how hard it must be to do that with one hand and one leg that you can't move no matter how hard you try.

Dad goes in to help, and I hear her slap away his hand and say, "Na!" I peek in and he's got her sitting on the edge of her bed but she's looking at him with narrowed eyes and she stays like that, mad at him for trying to help, for three long seconds. Then she reaches out with her left hand, grabs him by a suspender, and pulls him toward her for a quick hug.

"Na na na na na na na," she says, then pushes him away again and wags a finger near his face. And I know what she's saying—*Don't you go scaring me like that*—because she used to say that when I would fly down the street on Marcus's skateboard, dragging my toe to slow down while Marcus and Shane cheered me to go faster, faster.

I know exactly how Grandma feels. Like sometimes she wishes Dad weren't so brave like that. Brave like risk-your-life-whenever-the-sirens-sound brave.

I try to convince Grandma to come with us, to watch the parade and hear the music and eat funnel cake and fried Oreos, but she shoos us off and Dad says to come on, so I give her a big hug, an all-the-way-around hug, and before we leave Grandma slides *What's Going On* into its sleeve and presses it to my chest. "Na na."

When we get home, Dad says, "Quick. I don't want to be late." I run upstairs and take a shower, and even when I'm in my room, wrapped in my towel, I don't know if Dad is expecting me to come out dressed for the game and to give an apology to Coach Matthews and ask for my pinchy cleats and number eighty-eight jersey back and to line up with the B team to watch the game, or if he's expecting me to come out in my regular clothes to watch the reenactment from the top of the fire truck.

I just stand here and look into my drawer like I'm frozen again and can't even figure out what clothes to grab, but the longer I look down at that tight, shiny Under Armour shirt Dad got for me to wear beneath my uniform, the harder I can feel that *NO* sitting in my guts.

So I put on my shorts and my T-shirt and walk downstairs. Dad is pulling on his big boots and he's wearing his firefighter pants, suspenders up over his shoulders, and has his jacket tucked under his arm. All the firefighters go to Defeat of Jesse James Days in uniform. And even though he is brave like that, brave like wake-up-and-pull-on-a-uniform brave, I still manage to say, "I'm not playing, Dad. I quit for Parker, but I also quit for me."

He stands up and looks right at me, puts his hand on my shoulder, and nods. "I know."

That makes me feel like an entire pig pile has rolled off me and I can breathe again.

On the way to the firehouse we drive right past the restaurant and the humane society. The restaurant is still standing, but there are long licks of black char reaching up from the window and bits of siding have big burn holes right through. The yellow caution tape is still stretched around the site and a police car is parked outside.

The humane society doesn't look damaged at all and I crane my neck to check if the lights are on and I think there's someone moving around in there, and my heart aches to see Parker, and I hope they're giving the dogs a little extra breakfast this morning. I would.

Dad slows down and points to the blown-out restaurant window on the side of the building and starts telling me all the details. Everyone got out early and easy and they found the source right away: a grease trap in the kitchen that should have been cleaned out regularly. "It can just build up little by little without anyone really noticing," he says. "Then it's too late and everything nearby—parchment paper, foil, packaging materials, everything—is all just feeding the flames."

Roger has the truck out and ready when we get to the firehouse, and we all pile in and drive to the center of town. There are orange cones and a sign that says *Reserved for Firemen* in the same spot every year on Division Street. I'm thinking it's time to change that sign to *Firefighters*, and as soon as we park Sam hops off the engine and says she'll be back and I'm pretty sure she's going to see someone about that.

I take twenty dollars from Dad and run to get deep fried Oreos. The line is long and by the time I get back there's a piece of cardboard over *men* and in big black-Sharpied letters it reads *fighters*. I smile at Sam and she gives me a thumbs-up.

Dad and Sam are lifting little kids into the truck so they can pretend they're flying down the street to save the day. Roger rolls out a bit of hose and tells them how the stream is so powerful it takes a team to hold it steady.

The sun is warm, the air smells like cheese curds,

and the kids' faces are already sticky with blue cotton candy.

Then I hear, "Cy! Cy!" It's Eduardo, dressed in the band uniform: navy-blue pants and a white button-up shirt with Joseph Lee Heywood's face stitched in maroon over his heart. He's got a small music case that fits in his hand, and he's sprinting.

"I'm late for warm-ups! But hi!" he says as he runs up.

My hands are full of deep-fried Oreos, but I raise them up and kind of wave and say hi back.

"We're playing at halftime. Aren't you . . ." He makes the same gesture my grandma makes for football, cocking the black instrument case behind his head.

I shake my head. "I quit."

He nods and puts his hand out for a high five, and I kind of bobble the Oreos, so he puts out his elbow and we do this weird elbow-five thing. "Cool," he says.

"Wait, how are you already playing?" I gesture to his instrument. "Haven't you only had one practice?" I ask. "I thought it was just the seventh and eighth graders today."

Eduardo smiles and says, "I played oboe for two years at my old school. Mr. Fletcher said if I learned my part I could play. It's a pretty simple song." Then he waves bye and I tell him good luck and watch him run off on short, slow legs, tucking his oboe case toward his body like he's making a break for the end zone.

The kickoff to the Joseph Lee Heywood Middle School football game always starts right when the mob chases Jesse James and his gang out of the bank and down Division Street. The splintering sound of bullets from rifles held high overhead and horse hooves clacking and chasing the gang out of town are the signal for the referee to blow his whistle and the kicker to run in and kick.

I have the best seat in town because from the top of the truck I can see all the way down Division for the parade and reenactment and I can also see right over the middle school to the field where the A Team is jogging a warm-up lap with their heavy pads and wobbly helmets.

A big boom sounds and everyone cheers and the marching band starts stepping down the street. A tall man with a big drum on his belly waves his arms and *boom-boom*s, keeping rhythm as the trumpets squeal and flutes flitter, and when I see the line of oboes bobbing and buzzing I smile and think of Eduardo warming up for the game's halftime.

Dad and Leo and Roger and Sam climb up and join me on top of the truck.

This has always been my favorite part of the whole day, when the instruments parade through. Grandma used to dance and nudge me and I'd tap my foot with her up here on the fire truck with all the guys. Last year was the first year Grandma didn't come, and I danced a little, when the guys weren't looking, just for her.

I don't know who all those people are walking in the parade, waving and smiling and blowing kisses to the crowd. Maybe the mayor or governor or someone else really important. But I'm cheering for all the musicians with their red faces and puffed-out cheeks, and the rhythm I see bouncing in their shoulders. My foot taps harder against the truck's roof each time an instrument section adds in its sound and the music grows and trills down the street. And when the trombones start, I couldn't stop my feet from moving if I tried to. I can feel the music filling me up from ears to tapping toes, right through my pounding heart. Pounding, I swear, right on rhythm.

Leo sees me kind of dancing and gives me a little smile. It's not a real smile, though, it's a smile that looks down on me and makes me feel smaller than I already am. It's a smile that makes my feet go still. Then he claps my dad on the shoulder and nods in my direction. "Maybe he quit football for ballet?"

The trombone slides glide all the way down and back up and then *pop-pop-pop* with the trumpet squeals as they pass by the fire truck, and Dad leans in to Leo and says, loudly, "So what?"

And that gets my foot tapping again because I know he got that *So what?* from Grandma. And it shuts Leo right up.

As the music marches down the street, I eat another deep-fried Oreo in one bite and the melty middle makes me even more happy that I'm not sitting on the end of the football bench.

Then the horses come galloping and clacking, their riders' coattails flying in the wind as they race toward the bank. The crowd gasps at the gang riding by as if it were really 1876 and they don't already know the ending.

"Get 'em!" one man shouts.

Kids point to the horses as they zoom by.

The riders dismount and enter the bank, and that's when the gunshots start and I can see the teams line up on the middle school field.

Bang! Bang! Bang! And the gang flies back out of the bank and everyone in town knows what I know. Joseph Lee Heywood just refused to open the safe and is dead, but he will live on forever in our little town.

A mob of townsmen chase Jesse James and his gang down Division, firing their guns. *Bang! Bang! Bang!* And the kicker backs up and runs in and sends the ball flying through the air.

Clackety clackety clackety clack bang bang bang!

Someone catches the ball and runs five yards with it before the crack of helmets echoes with gunshots and he's on the bottom of a pile.

The crowd roars and gives their mightiest Heywood Hurrahs and starts folding up their chairs and making their way from Division Street to the football game.

"What happens next?" Sam asks. I forgot that this is her first Defeat of Jesse James Days.

"We watch the middle school game, then the high school game, let kids sit in the truck, eat cheese curds . . ." Roger says.

"No, I mean with those guys." She points to the riders, bullets still cracking against the sky. "Do they catch them all?"

My dad nods. "Yep. After a couple weeks and four hundred miles."

"You're kidding," she says. "Just the townspeople?"

My dad nods. "That Joseph Lee Heywood started something when he said no."

And I never really thought about it that way before. That Joseph Lee Heywood was brave and gave everyone around him the time they needed to be brave too. To get their guns and jump on their horses and ride and ride until the bad guys stopped.

CHAPTER 21

An Olson

My book review is almost done. The internet has tons of short write-ups and easy-to-understand summaries of *Wonder*. I even find one that uses a quote and tells me what happens in the end. When I put everything in my own words and print out a color picture of the book cover, my review looks really good, so good not even Mr. Hewett and his excellent fake detector would be able to tell that I'm still only on page twenty-eight. But it's due in two days, and even if the only thing I do from now to then is read and sway and slow down and think like Grandma showed me, I wouldn't be far enough to hand in a review without a fake.

This is the first year we get letter grades in school, and I'm pretty sure this book review could get an A.

Dad pops in to say good night and ask what part of the reenactment was my favorite, which is our own little Defeat of Jesse James Days tradition. I always say the Oreos. And we laugh and he says that those deep-fried Oreos are just as important to this town as Joseph Lee Heywood or any of the townsmen that chased Jesse James out.

This year, though, I say something different when he asks.

"The music," I say. "The trombones."

He sits down on the edge of my bed and says, "Is that right?"

"Sorry it's not football," I say.

Dad shakes his head. "I'm not."

"But I'm an Olson," I tell him. "I'm supposed to be a wide receiver. Number eighty-eight."

He's looking me right in the eyes, and I'm thinking that he might be just like Grandma, and if he looks long enough he'll see deep down in and learn the rest of my secrets. And I wonder if he can see that my guts are still tied in knots about Marcus and Shane and Eduardo, and that my heart hurts a little bit every beat that I'm apart from Parker, and I wonder if he can look into my very cells right to where the Olson gene is supposed to be and see what I have there instead.

"You"—his voice is kind of cracky-shaky, but he

raises a big finger and points it right at my chest—"are not *supposed* to be anything but you." He clears his voice and blinks his eyes. "And when I look at you, I don't want to see me. I want to see *you*." He taps his finger against my chest again.

That makes my voice kind of cracky-shaky too, but I say, "Good. Because I don't look anything like you." We both laugh a little and he tousles my fuzzy curls with his big hand.

"Now get some sleep." He turns out my light and stands up. My bed lets up from the weight of him lifting off.

He stops at the door. "And you *are* an Olson," he says. "You were an Olson when you cried louder than the sirens for a five-alarm fire, you were an Olson when you pushed away baby food and went straight for my burger, and you were an Olson when you quit football. You just are," he says. "No matter what you do."

He closes the door and I close my eyes and listen to my heartbeat, *one-and-two-and-three-and-four-and*, and I try to think how I can convince him before Monday that Parker is an Olson too.

CHAPTER 22

Right Where I Belong

Dad gets called into work on Sunday to finish reports and sign papers and talk to people about the fire on Friday at the pizza restaurant, which means I don't have any chance to convince him that we should be at the humane society on Monday morning. That we should skip work and skip school and get there before they open, before they can load Parker into a van and take him an hour away from me.

Dad says I can come to the firehouse if I stay upstairs and do my homework. I already finished my math at Grandma's and my book review is ready to go even though it's not due until Tuesday, but I slide *Wonder* in my book bag and think maybe I can read a couple pages, stopping and thinking and finding the rhythm. Maybe

Auggie can keep my mind off Parker until Dad is done at work.

The restaurant owner and manager and all the workers show up at the firehouse and sit around the kitchen table with Chief Reynolds and my dad and Sam and Officer Wilson. I can hear them talking about whose responsibility it is to clean out the grease traps and how could everyone just let it go and go like that? The schedules they kept hanging in the kitchen have burned, and as workers come in to answer questions, they just keep saying they thought the other person was going to do it.

"That's a dangerous thought," my dad says. "That someone else is going to do it, so you're off the hook."

Then Officer Wilson and Chief Reynolds write down all the facts for the insurance company, and it feels like it's taking forever and ever. I want to see Parker. I want to run to the humane society, even though they're probably not open because it's Sunday, and even though my dad says that seeing him will only make it harder.

But so what?

I can at least go and check if maybe someone forgot to lock the door when they were leaving yesterday, or peek in the windows to see if I can catch a glimpse of anyone going in to feed the dogs.

I can at least try.

I can't wait anymore, so I pack up my book bag and

run down the stairs and even though it's not like me to interrupt, I say, "Dad, I have to go."

He looks up from the table in the firehouse kitchen where Officer Wilson is jotting in a notepad. He doesn't say anything, but his eyes are warning me.

"Parker's leaving tomorrow for another shelter far from here," I say. "It's just what you do. For family." I take a breath that raises my shoulders up. "You let them stick their nose on your shoulder one last time. Or at least you try."

Dad's eyes change. They stop squinting and get softer and he purses his lips into a little understanding kind of smile and nods like he's saying *OK, then.*

I'm sort of half running because I want to get there fast and hug Parker, but my legs automatically slow down when I get to the restaurant. I peek over the yellow caution tape and look in through the burned-out windows to the charred kitchen.

Usually that kitchen is busy with bakers tossing pizza dough in the air and catching them on their forearms and waiters going in and out with hot plates and bubbling pitchers of soda.

It looks emptier than empty in there—sad and damaged and hollow—and I wish there were some kind of instant replay where you could jump in and change what happened before, so that all the workers could take a second and check the grease trap and clean it out and not just think that someone else would. That way, Dad wouldn't have to be at the firehouse filing papers and I could be convincing him that a dog would make our family even better and then we could eat pizza and drink soda like we do lots of Sundays.

The sign hanging on the humane society says *Closed*. The door is locked and the blinds are pulled down, but if I put my face close to the glass and close one eye I can peek between the blinds, and I see someone moving inside.

Bang! Bang! Bang! I knock until one of the vet techs I recognize lifts the blinds. When she sees me she gives me a look like I should know better, but I think she should know better too than to expect I wouldn't show up the day before Parker has to move.

She cracks the door. "Where's Max?" I ask.

"It's Sunday," she says.

"It's Parker's last day," I respond.

She opens the door wider. "Two minutes, Cyrus."

I step in and say thanks and it feels a little strange being here without The 7. I miss inching into their circle and sharing leashes and laughing and saying, "See you next time."

The vet tech makes her way down the hallway. I hear

a kennel lock squeak open and I hear Parker yip and the other dogs bark and then I see him running down the hall, a big brown blurry panting mess that lands right on my shoulder.

"Hey, buddy," I whisper and scratch him behind the ears the way he likes. I whisper that he'll find a new home soon and someone will love him as much as I do and maybe I can convince Dad to drive an hour for a walk sometime and that he can keep my T-shirt.

When it's been two minutes, the vet tech reminds me that it's time to go, so I stand up slowly and Parker whimpers and I do too and it makes sense now, what my Dad said about getting too attached, because when I step away from Parker it feels like something inside me catches and burns and I feel emptier than a scorched-out kitchen.

I move toward the door and push it open fast and I almost tumble right out because there on the other side is my dad and he's pulling as I'm pushing again and I fall right into him and I don't even try not to cry. I cry and cry and pound my fists on his suspender-strapped chest and tell him it's not right. That Parker was all alone and scared on my birthday and he found me because he was supposed to find me and I'm not supposed to let him go like this.

I sniff my nose and clear my throat to say more, but Dad says something first.

"So go get him."

I look at him and he juts his chin in through the door.

"Go on."

And before I know it, Dad is talking with the vet tech at the front desk, and she's telling him that they don't process adoptions on Sundays, but my dad is saying it would save us the trip to wherever they're taking Parker tomorrow and couldn't she walk us through the process now? I'm hugging and patting Parker and he's wagging his tail so hard I'm pretty sure he's going to pee on my toe-scuffed Vans but not even that could make me back up a step. The vet tech sighs and starts showing Dad different papers and explaining how pet adoption works and Parker's head is back on my shoulder and I'm crying big happy sploshy tears all over his fur and he's panting sloppy strings of spit on my shirt and I know that this is right where I belong.

CHAPTER 23

So What?

Parker sleeps in my room, curled up on the bottom of my bed, right on my feet, all night. I wake up from him pawing his way up the comforter, sniffing in my ear, and patting my chest with his paw.

"Morning, Parker," I say. "Parker Olson."

Dad makes me go to school even though I want to stay home with Parker. But he says he'll come home at lunch to let him out, and he promises me he'll scratch him behind the ears.

I leave him curled up in the living room with my T-shirt and tell him I'll be home after school.

Dad says he'll drive me today, so I hop in the car and rub my hands together while he starts the engine. Sometimes it seems like fall starts faster than a snap to the quarterback, and instead of summer tans and T-shirts, it's wind and leaves and jackets with hoods. This morning is the snap, and just like that, I'm rubbing my hands together and wishing the car would heat up faster.

The drive is short, but Dad waits until we're almost there to say, "I don't like what you told me about Marcus and Shane being mean to that new kid."

"Eduardo," I say.

"Eduardo."

"I don't like it either." The car is just starting to get warm as we pull up to the front of the school, and now I really don't want to get out.

"Good," Dad says. "I trust you'll know what to do then."

I nod and say OK because I do know what I should do, I'm just not sure I'm brave like that. Brave like snuff-out-a-fire-before-it-spreads kind of brave.

The hallway is clogged with kids opening and closing their lockers and talking about the football game and how a freshman threw the winning touchdown. They're all looking for Marcus, but I'm looking for any of The 7, and when I see Katherine and Ruth and Alexis talking across the hall I jump above all the heads between us and wave my arms and I don't care how dorky I look. When that doesn't work, I make myself small, Eduardo small, hunched-over-and-weave-between-everyone small.

"You, guys!" I burst as soon as I get to them. "Parker!" And in one long breath, I tell them all about running to the humane society and the vet tech letting me in and Dad and the adoption and how Parker's at home right now. My home. Our home.

By then the rest of The 7 is circled around and Elli says, "Yes!" and gives me a high five and people stare at us but we don't care. Lou puts her arm around my shoulders and gives me a hug and June reaches out so we can connect fists.

I tell them that I'm still going to go to the humane society with them sometimes to walk the other dogs. I like helping. I like their circle.

Then someone shouts, "There he is!" and he's pointing at Marcus, who's sauntering toward Mr. Hewett's room wearing his jersey. Everyone starts giving him a "Heywood Hurrah! Heywood Hurrah!" And it doesn't feel right, him getting any Heywood Hurrahs, because he's not brave like that. Brave like stare-down-what's-wrong-and-stand-up-for-what's-right brave.

The teachers start calling for us all to keep it moving and get to homeroom, so I duck and weave back across the hall to my locker.

Marcus is making his way down the hallway. I hide behind the open door of my locker and fake that I'm looking for something way in the back because I don't want them to ask me about quitting the team and I wonder if we're even friends without football, but when they pass by, Marcus says, "Hey, where were you? What happened?"

And Shane adds, "Yeah, did you really quit?"

I nod and I clench my teeth closed so I don't say sorry.

They just kind of shrug and say, "OK," and, "That stinks," and then walk into Mr. Hewett's room.

Eduardo shows up at the bottom of our locker. He's squatting down on flat feet, his knees bent up to his ears, and he's organizing his notebooks.

"Morning!" he says. His oboe case sticks out of his book bag.

"Nice job," I tell him. "Halftime was really the best part of the whole game."

Eduardo laughs a little and says, "Don't tell Marcus that."

We close the locker and Alejandro comes over and reaches out for a high five and it kind of makes me wish I had a brother too, or maybe it just makes me miss Parker even though he's at home and I get to see him later.

Eduardo and I walk into Mr. Hewett's room and I sit with him again at Patrick and Curtis's table. Everyone is zipping their bags and talking about our book reviews that are due tomorrow and a math test we have at the end of the week so I'm not sure if anybody else hears it, but I do.

I hear Marcus describing his game-winning throw. How he had to hold the ball and wait until he saw an opening and how he held on even when he was *this close* to getting tackled right before halftime.

He clears his throat and whispers to Shane, "Then little Edweirdo Button came out on the field with his Velcro shoes to play his *oboe*." Shane laughs first and then it spreads to Zander's table and Geordie and Chris are chuckling because the way he said *oboe* made it sound like it was directly the opposite of being brave like that. Brave like throw-a-ball-before-you-get-mowed-over brave.

And it's not.

And I can hear Benji kind of chuckle and say "He plays the *oboe*?"

And I know what I have to do. Put the fire out at its source because it's spreading to Zander and Chris and Benji and pretty soon our whole class will be in flames.

So I stand up and point myself in their direction and clear my throat and say, "So what?"

Everyone stops chuckling and looks up at me.

"What, Cy?" Marcus says.

Now it's really quiet, but the embers are still glowing

and even though they're not roaring and flaming I know how hot those little bits can be and I know all they want is to find some loose paper to start back up again.

I will not be loose paper.

"I said, 'So what'?"

I say it to Marcus and to the whole class.

Shane shifts in his seat and looks like he's trying to find something to say. Like Marcus has the ball and it's his job to deflect all the tackles, so he kind of sputters out, "The oboe is weird."

"So what?" I repeat.

And no one has a good answer because there isn't one. So what if there's Velcro on his shoes? And so what if he plays the oboe? So what if he isn't even tall enough to reach Shane's shoulder? Or thinks a picture book about a boy who likes to dance is the best he's ever read? So what?

And then the coolest thing happens. *I* start to catch because Addison says, "Yeah, so what?" and turns around to look at Marcus and Shane and Zander. "I'm weird too. I have teal streaks in my hair."

"Me too!" Hadleigh says and yanks on her ponytail.

"Yeah, so what?" Nora adds. "I like to color my fingernails with Sharpies. That's kind of weird."

Eduardo pipes up and fans out his fingers. "Can you do mine?" And everyone kind of giggles, but not *at*

Eduardo like before, more *with* him because he's funny and doesn't care if others think his rainbow-Sharpied fingernails are weird.

Then Patrick pipes up too and says, "Yeah, so what? I dress up my hamsters and let them run through my sister's dollhouse!" This makes everyone laugh even harder, and Patrick is laughing so hard that he kind of chokes out, "But so what? So what?"

And before I know it, everyone is trying to outweird everyone else.

"I wear something green to school every single day! If I don't, I feel itchy all over."

"You do?" a few people respond.

Chris puts his foot up on his desk and pulls up his jeans. "See!" His socks are lime green. "Tomorrow I'm wearing green boxers! I'm obsessed with green! But so what?"

"I like memorizing dates and maps!"

"I can't ride a bike!"

"I have a math tutor!"

And with all the *So what?*s crackling around the room and people standing up and showing off their weird, without even trying, I pipe up and say that I'm weird too. That I sound good when I read out loud, but it's impossible to keep a story in my brain and I'm going to sign up for band and play the trombone because it's the coolest sound in the whole world.

"The trombone?" Shane asks, and he says it like Marcus said *oboe*.

"So what?" Eduardo says.

"Yeah, so what?" a few people respond together and it makes them laugh again.

Mr. Hewett is clapping his hands three times and raising his peace fingers in the air, trying to get us to be quiet, but a few more people say, "I'm afraid of swimming!" and "I can't ride in a car for more than ten minutes without puking!"

I'm kind of feeling sad for Marcus and Shane, who are sitting in the back with pink glowing beneath their cheeks, because I know they're weird too, because they've been my friends forever. Shane still plays with G.I. Joes and Marcus cries at the end of movies all the time. And so what? But they aren't adding their weird to the room, so I just kind of smile at them and sit down next to Eduardo, who pushes his arm over a little into mine until our elbows touch.

"*Gracias*," he whispers.

At the end of homeroom I ask Mr. Hewett if I can borrow *Red*. I have all this good so-what feeling stirring in my belly, so I just come right out with it and I tell him I haven't finished any books, not really, ever. I tell him about my grandma and how she helps me find the rhythm and how I might not be able to finish *Wonder*, at least not yet, but I like *Red*, and I think I can write a pretty good review.

Mr. Hewett says he has some strategies for me to try, and that I should be proud I can read so fluently, and that I'm brave for telling him.

I call Dad from the office at the end of the day and he shows up in Mr. Fletcher's band room to sign a permission slip and fill out a rental form for my very own trombone. Mr. Fletcher tells my dad we'll be working on the basics for the first few weeks: buzzing into the mouthpiece, playing notes, reading a simple song and practicing it over and over again.

"Students who are ready will play that song at the football game Thursday," he says. "But there's no pressure." Dad thanks him and shakes his hand and asks me if I can carry that big case all the way to the firehouse after band practice. I nod my head.

"OK, then," he says, and taps the case. "I wonder what Parker will think of this."

We both laugh a little and I'm imagining Parker's head parked on one shoulder and my trombone parked on the other and that gets my foot tapping.

CHAPTER 24

First Book

After band practice, I run faster than I've ever run before, even with my big trombone case banging against my leg. I run like I'm being chased by a hundred cornerbacks and safeties, but this time I don't want to fumble the ball so I can stop the play and avoid the hit. I want to keep running all the way to the firehouse so I can tell Dad everything about my first band practice. How I buzzed the mouthpiece right on the first try and learned how to connect the slide to the bell and how even though I'm small I'm not too small to stretch my arm all the way down to the seventh position. I think I might even tell him that I'm not the best at reading books yet, but I think I'm going to be OK at reading music because when I see a note on the staff I can *hear* it too and that's easier to remember than just words and words.

And I can't wait to see my dog.

Dad is ready to go when I get there, and Leo is coming in for the night shift. He takes one look at my trombone and I'm almost hoping he says something because I've got a big *So what?* waiting for him. He kind of smirks a smile and says he'll be upstairs lifting weights. And in that second I realize that if kids like Marcus and Shane just keep sparking little fires without anyone saying *NO* to them or *So what?* to them they'll probably end up like Leo. Someone who cares too much about lockers and walks around like he's a little bigger than everyone else.

But something tells me that Sam is working on snuffing out his sparks and Dad is catching on too. And they're good firefighters.

Before Dad can put the car in park in our driveway, I open my door and fly out and fumble with the key and push open the door and Parker is right there waiting for me and we're both wagging and huffing and squealing and I still can't believe he's my dog.

I get his leash and take him outside and toss him my old, deflated pee-wee football in the yard, and it reminds me of when football was fun, slow and easy, with no chance of getting plowed into the ground. Parker runs long across the grass and looks back, tracking the ball. He catches it every time and brings it back and drops it right at my feet, wagging his tail for more, and I'm thinking he's definitely an Olson.

Dad calls us in for dinner and we measure out a cup of the food the veterinarian told us to buy and fill up Parker's water bowl. He eats fast, then curls under the table at my feet while Dad and I have spaghetti and meatballs. Dad looks at him and kind of smiles and I know what he's thinking. He's thinking this isn't so bad, having a dog around.

"What do you have for homework?" he asks.

"Practice my trombone for twenty minutes," I tell him and I run quick to the mudroom to get my book bag so I can show him how the music looks on the page: round black notes on five solid lines. I point my finger and sing how the notes should sound.

"You can read that?" Dad asks.

I nod. "Mr. Fletcher says I'm a natural."

Dad chuckles and looks back down at the music. "You get that from your grandma."

I look at Dad with a face like *Duh* and it makes us laugh, but really I'm thinking that I wish I had listened earlier to the notes that Grandma gave me. The round black notes lodged way deep down in, down where all my secrets sat, beneath heavy shoulder pads and unread books, deep where Grandma could see if she looked me right in my eyes.

"What else you got in there?" And for one second I think he means deep in my guts, but he's pointing to my book bag.

I pull out my math notebook and show him the problems I did in class. Then he sees the book review with the fancy color-printed cover. "This looks nice." He flips the cover and reads the first paragraph. "Sounds like you liked the book."

I could just say *Yeah* and tell him about how Auggie didn't fit in at first and how even his best friend made fun of him behind his back once and how it all seemed so real, like it could happen at my school. Like it was happening at my school. But the music is playing in me loud and Parker is shifting his weight on my feet and I know I'm done with fakes.

"I'm actually going to rewrite it." I take it from his hands.

He raises his eyebrows.

I take a deep breath and let my big secret rise up from my belly and tell him I didn't really read *Wonder*, and I tell him about all the reading fakes I've been doing for as long as I can remember, and that Mr. Hewett and I are going to meet at lunch tomorrow and practice some strategies and Eduardo's going to come too, just because he's a good friend.

Dad's eyes look sad and it looks like he's thinking about a whole lot, but all he says is, "I'm sorry," and, "Thanks for telling me." Then he smiles and adds, "And I like this Eduardo."

I smile back and nod. "Me too."

Dad takes a long last drink of water and starts loading the dishes into the dishwasher. "But isn't the review due tomorrow?" he asks.

That's when I pull out *Red* and tell him my plan. That I can't read all of *Wonder* yet, but I know I can read this one. "Mr. Hewett read it to our class, so I already know I like it."

Dad closes the dishwasher and comes to sit next to me and I'm wondering if he's going to say I can't write my first sixth-grade book report on a picture book about crayons. But he reaches out his big hand and taps the cover just like Grandma does. "Read it to me."

I open the cover and read the first page, and as soon as I do, Parker gets up and puts his head in my lap so he can see the pictures too. I read the words easily, and I like their rhythm. And after each two pages I stop and think and explain to Parker what I read.

Dad is nodding and following along and I think he might even like the book too, because at the end he says, "Who says strawberries can't be blue?"

* * *

That night, I go to bed with my trombone case tucked in beside me—which is totally weird, but so what?—and Parker asleep at my feet and I'm feeling like I'm right where I belong.

CHAPTER 25

Kindness

In homeroom the next day, everyone is gathered around Hadleigh because she's coloring Eduardo's fingernails with purple and orange Sharpies and Chris is pointing to the band of his boxers saying, "See! I told you! Green!"

There is a still a murmur of what happened yesterday and every once in a while I hear someone say, "Weird!" or "So what?"

I give Eduardo a high five when Hadleigh finishes his nails, and when I look back at Marcus and Shane I smile and say hi. I'm expecting them to roll their eyes or call me Oliver Button, but they don't. They just kind of wave and say, "What's up?" and I wonder if maybe they're done poking fun at Eduardo, and me for being friends with him. And I wonder if sometime they'll want to come throw the football with Parker and me in the backyard.

And I don't know if it's because by the end of the day most of the class has rainbow-colored fingernails, or because we all know how weird we all really are, but things feel different and better, and even having lunch with Mr. Hewett to talk about how hard reading is doesn't feel so bad. Eduardo sits right next to me as Mr. Hewett reads a page aloud and stops to tell me what his brain is thinking after every couple of sentences. I kind of like practicing with them, and Mr. Hewett says we can do it again tomorrow.

In English class we all take out our book reviews and pens and notebooks, and when we're all ready and quiet, Mr. Hewett calls us to the rug for our book of the day.

He shows us the cover of the book, *Each Kindness*, and starts to read us a story about a new girl named Maya. Mr. Hewett is reading with a soft voice and everyone on the rug is leaning in. Chloe, the girl telling the story, and all the other kids in class aren't nice to Maya and one day Maya just doesn't come to school. She moved, and now Chloe can't ever say sorry or start being nicer, and it's too late for the other kids to stand up and say NO. Mr. Hewett shows us the pictures slowly and my heart sinks and I lower my head and scooch an inch closer to Eduardo on the rug. I look back to see if Marcus' and Shane's heads are lowered too. They are.

When we return to our seats, Mr. Hewett asks us to take out our book reviews and pass them forward. He collects them in a big stack in his hands and says, "I can't wait to read all of these." Then he walks around and sticks one yellow Post-it note on each desk and projects the directions up on the SMART Board.

"In a moment you will receive another student's book review," he says. "When you finish reading it, you'll jot something kind to the writer on this Post-it note and stick it to their paper."

No one has any questions, so Mr. Hewett begins walking around the room handing our book reviews back out. I'm trying to see where mine is in the stack and whose desk it'll land on, but I can't tell. Then he slides Geordie's on my table and it's all typed up and in a fancy plastic report cover and across the top it says, *The Best Book Ever: Because of Winn-Dixie.* I have to check the name again and make sure it says *Geordie Seavers,* because I've been in Geordie's class for three years in a row and everyone knows he barely talks and when he does, it's usually about video games. And I was in his fourth-grade class when we read *Because of Winn-Dixie* and I don't think he raised his hand once the whole time. There's a movie for *Winn-Dixie.* I loved it.

I read his review slowly and stop to think after each sentence. It mostly tells what the book is about, but at the end it says, *I read this with my class in fourth grade, but then I read it again last year by myself and made my mom read it too. I was trying to convince her to get me a dog and this book is what made her say OK. That is why it's the best book ever. PS: My dog's name is Lucy.*

On the Post-it note I write:

Geordie—I liked your review. That book was hard when we read it in fourth grade, but I want to try again. I have a dog named Parker. We should all play sometime.—Cyrus

Mr. Hewett asks if everyone is done reading and jotting and begins collecting the reviews again. He asks Addison and Zander to help him pass them back out to the writers so we can all see our comments. Zander lays mine on my desk. It doesn't look as fancy as Geordie's in his plastic report cover, but I'm feeling proud of it anyway. It's a book I actually read. It's a review I actually wrote. No fakes. The yellow Post-it note is stuck in the bottom right corner.

Cy—I didn't know a picture book could mean anything, but I guess you're right. Who cares if he draws red or blue?—Marcus

I look back at Marcus and he gives me a dorky thumbs-up and smiles. Then I catch Geordie looking at me and he kind of pants like a dog and lets out a little bark, which is kind of weird, but so what? So I pant and bark back, and I'm pretty sure that means we're going to get Lucy and Parker together to play.

The bell rings and Mr. Hewett tells us to leave our reviews on the table so he can read them and create our first class book of reviews.

As we stand up to go, everything in Mr. Hewett's room feels easier and better and hard to describe, but I'm not worrying that anyone is laughing behind my back or saying something about me writing about a picture book. And I'm hoping that when we go into the hallway that feeling comes with us. And it does, because the first people I see are DeeDee and June and Katherine and they wave big across the hall and call, "Hey, Cy! How's Parker?" I give a thumbs-up and head toward my locker to get my trombone for band practice.

Toward the end of band, I actually have to go to the bathroom and I wish I didn't because I love buzzing into the mouthpiece and hearing the sounds blast out of the big bell. So I'm hurrying down the hall when I see the student achievement board outside our homeroom, next to the sports trophy case where my dad's football picture hangs. Mr. Hewett has already stapled new work to the board and right there in the center is my book review and my name is printed out on a big card and stapled above it. Cyrus Olson.

The Best Book I've Ever Read: Red
By Cyrus Olson

The best book I've ever read is a picture book called *Red: A Crayon's Story.* I know that seems kind of weird because I'm in sixth grade and supposed to have read a hundred really awesome books by now. But reading is hard and this book made sense and stayed in my brain.

Plus, Red is a little like me. He's supposed to be drawing red strawberries and red fire trucks, but no matter how hard he tries everything comes out blue. I think everyone has a color inside that they have to find and then everyone else needs to just let them be that color. Like me. I'm Cyrus Olson, foot tapper, dog lover, trombone blaster.

CHAPTER 26

Standing Ovation

All I've done for the two days is practice this one song over and over again in my bedroom at night with Parker as my audience. I play it in my head at dinner, I tap my feet to the tune in every class, and sometimes without me even trying my arm raises right up on its own and practices the positions on the slide.

It's the school song about being brave and it's only two lines long and the trombone part only has four different notes the whole song, but I practice and practice until I play it perfectly for Mr. Fletcher and he says, "Olson. You're ready to play with us at Thursday's game."

When Thursday comes, even though I have the song memorized and it'll be over in thirty seconds, my knees are still shaking harder than they ever shook when I was actually on the field as a wide receiver with everyone cheering for me to "Put your head down" and "Run, run, run!" But I can't help it. My knees shake and my mouth feels dry and there are only eleven parents so far who have taken their seats on the bleachers but it feels like the Super Bowl.

I can feel Great-Grandpa Olson's dog tags beneath my shirt, and I try to steady my breathing, thinking about his name and blood type rising and falling, rising and falling, on my chest.

Dad's on duty today, but he's taking a break from the firehouse to watch the band. He walks over in his suspenders and big pants and starts chatting with Shane's mom. He points to me and I kind of wave and it makes my cheeks feel hot but it also makes me feel good, like Dad can see my real color deep down in.

My music stand is perched in front of me, and when I look at the notes they sing right back. I know this song. I know it.

Dad keeps looking toward the parking lot and at his watch and I know he has to get back to the firehouse, so I wish Mr. Fletcher would hurry up so we could play and be done and then the team could kick off.

There are three eighth-grade girls who are standing around a microphone, ready to sing. Eduardo's sitting in the first row of the band risers with the other oboes and flutes and I'm right between two other seventh graders with trombones. And I'm thinking, there's no faking the trombone. There's no pretending to read the music and play because when the trombone slides go out and back, mine better be right there with them.

Seven more people wearing Heywood colors, including Alejandro, show up and find seats in the bleachers. Mr. Fletcher taps his baton against his music stand and welcomes the crowd.

Dad looks toward the parking lot again and stands up and waves his hand kind of secretly like he's saying *Hurry* to someone over there. Then he calls out and asks Mr. Fletcher if he wouldn't mind waiting one minute and now everyone is looking at him and I stand up and crane my neck to see who it is.

That's when I see the van from Grandma's assisted-living building in the handicapped spot and Grandma in a wheelchair going down the electric lift. Milly is waiting for her on the curb and so is the whole firehouse. Roger and Leo and Sam and even Mike are here, and when I see them I look at Dad and my eyes start to burn and the music notes start to look blurry and I'm glad I have them memorized.

Dad rushes to help wheel Grandma in but when she

gets closer I hear her say, "Na!" and I know what she's doing, because I know my grandma. She's pushing herself up and out of the chair and walking the last few steps on her own two feet.

With Milly on one side and Dad on the other, she steps carefully and finds a seat on the first bleacher. She looks for me and catches my eye and says, "Na na na na." And I know what she's saying because she used to say it all the time when she showed up to football games or parent teacher conferences. *Not for the world.*

She'd never miss this.

My dad and the rest of the firehouse shuffle behind them to the second bleacher and Mr. Fletcher smiles and turns to us and lifts his baton, which means *Get your instruments ready.*

The team is lined up on the sideline and Marcus and Shane give me a little nod before they put on their helmets.

I bring the mouthpiece to my lips and watch Mr. Fletcher's baton go up and down and left and right and one-and-two-and-three-and-four-and . . . And then I'm playing and Sam is nodding and my Grandma's left foot is tapping and she's closing her eyes like I'm playing "Somewhere Over the Rainbow" instead of a simple song about being brave and playing hard. I look from her to the notes and back to her, then to the notes again. And I can't help but think that Dad is right. I got this from Grandma, and it's our language.

The song is over fast. We leave our instruments in playing position until Mr. Fletcher brings down his baton. There's a moment of silence, then the crowd applauds and Marcus and Shane start to clap on the sideline and the rest of the team follows. It's already feeling good. Good like skip-a-football-practice-to-run-to-Parker good.

But then this thing happens. Grandma inches to the edge of the bleacher and starts to push up. She wobbles a little and puts her left hand on Milly's shoulder to steady herself, but she's up. And she's cheering, "Na na na na!" and clapping her left hand against the right one, which is curled in, unmoving, to her body.

And then Dad stands too. And before I know it the applause is longer than the whole song and Leo is the next to stand. He looks right at me and nods and claps and goes, "Heywood Hurrah!"

And I can't help but think of the end of *Wonder*. I know from my fake book review research that Auggie gets a standing ovation in the end, and that he thinks that everyone should get a standing ovation at least once in their life. I even used that quote in my fake book review.

There are only eighteen parents, one Alejandro, one grandma, one Milly, and four firefighters in the audience, but it feels bigger, because I know what my grandma and dad are standing and cheering for, and it's not just for the four notes I played on the trombone.

They're standing because I did something real. No fakes. Just Cyrus. Cyrus Olson.

And I might not be brave like bottom-of-a-pig-pile brave, but I am brave. Brave like Eduardo brave. And brave like Sam brave. Brave like stand-up-and-say-NO brave, and brave like Oliver Button brave.

Brave like show-up-and-be-you brave.

Brave like Grandma brave.

That night Dad lets me sleep over at the firehouse, even though it's a school night, and he lets Parker come too. We make grilled cheese sandwiches and drink chocolate milk and watch the Vikings play the Packers with Parker right there on the couch between us.

Parker flinches at the hard tackles too and I pat his back and tell him it's OK and let him rest his head on my shoulder.

We talk a little about the new reading teacher Mr. Hewett introduced me to and how Dad is going in for a conference next week and how normally I wouldn't want to work one-on-one with her at all but now I do because I want to read *Wonder* and *Because of Winn-Dixie.*

Then he starts telling me about August twenty-seventh eleven years ago. "I never told you this part of the story," he says. "Because it's the scary part." I look up at him and he tells me that there was a waiting period where my birth parents could have shown up and taken me back. "I had already held you and named you," he says and his eyes get all watery. "I couldn't imagine having to let you go."

He pats my hand on Parker's back.

"Is that why you didn't want me to—" I pet Parker's back again.

"Get too attached," he says. "But I knew from the moment he put his head on your shoulder he was your dog."

He gives me a big all-the-way-around kind of hug with Parker right in the middle, and he holds on for an extra second before whispering in my ear, "Now, let's go, Vikings."

Between plays we talk about other stuff. Like Eduardo and Alejandro and how even though they're twins, they don't look alike and they aren't good at the same things and how that's kind of like me being an Olson.

"But both those boys are kind," Dad says. "And you are as Olson as it gets."

I look at us, both with our feet stretched out to the

coffee table and crossed at the ankle and each with one hand on Parker between us. "See?" he says.

We laugh a little and watch the wide receiver run it in for a touchdown, and I know that here is right where I belong.

AUTHOR'S NOTE

Brave Like That takes place in the real town of North-field, Minnesota, where I attended undergrad at Carleton College.

While I hope I remain true to the spirit of the town, I have taken some liberties to fictionalize certain aspects of Northfield for the sake of the story, the largest of which is how fiercely the town rallies around the brav-ery of Joseph Lee Heywood. While Defeat of Jesse James Days is a real days-long event that occurs each Septem-ber in Northfield, I exaggerated the town's idolization of Joseph Lee Heywood, the banker who wouldn't open the safe for Jesse James and his gang.

I hope the small inconsistencies don't detract from the overall essence of Northfield, a town to which I feel a great tie. And yes, the Malt-O-Meal factory does make the whole town smell like the most incredible fresh-baked Cheerios.

I'm also sending a huge, happy shout-out to all the teachers and librarians and caretakers of all kinds who read, daily, to kids. In *Brave Like That*, Cyrus's teacher participates in something called #classroombookaday, which is a real-life effort created by Jillian Heise, who was inspired by Donalyn Miller's #bookaday. It's a huge part of Cyrus's personal growth and the culture shift in his class. It is so encouraging to know that the daily sharing of stories is happening in classrooms all over the country. For more information, visit www.classroombookaday.com, follow @heisereads on Twitter and Instagram, and check out her blog at www.heisereads.com.

ACKNOWLEDGMENTS

During the writing of *Brave Like That*, Kamahnie and I moved from New York City to Vermont with our one-and-a-half-year-old son and infant daughter. And I didn't think I was brave like that. Brave like pack-up-your-apartment-and-move-states-with-two-babies-while-writing-a-book brave. It was exciting and filled with happiness, but like all transitions, it took time to find my footing and keep my momentum with writing. I simply could not have written this book without the help of the many big-hearted people who supported us through the move and encouraged me to keep going. Word by word I found Cyrus's voice again, and his story, and I got my groove back with a new process in a new place.

I owe this first to my parents—you are exceptionally generous of spirit and time and I am beyond fortunate to have such nurturing, steady, and kind people in my life. Thank you, endlessly, for everything.

Kelley Hackett and Heather Mayo—you are pure magic. It made me a better writer to know that while I was focused on Cyrus, Miles and Paige were happily covered in mud and hugs. Thank you.

To Kevin Clayton and the whole crew at Village Wine and Coffee and to Elizabeth Bluemle and the whole crew at the Flying Pig Bookstore in Shelburne—your spaces are so inviting, full of community, and charm, and at-home feeling. Thank you for your support.

I am so grateful for Candas Pinar, Adriana Saipe, and Becca Taudien—my writer-artist-friends. My mom-friends. My friend-friends. It's a special thing to find people like you.

My agent, Stephen Barbara, is a constant, reassuring partner in my writing, and a fan of Cyrus right from the beginning. I have leaned on him so many times throughout the process, and he is always, always right there.

My editor, Erica Sussman, worked so hard to help me tighten the strings of Cyrus's story. She has the most incredible ear. From big picture to small detail, I have learned so much over the course of three books and am still just so proud to work with her.

And to everyone at HarperCollins who had a hand in turning my manuscript into the beautiful book it is now, thank you for the care you have taken, Louisa Currigan, Chris Kwon, Alison Donalty, Ann Dye, Meaghan Finnerty, Olivia Russo, Rebecca McGuire, Patty Rosati, Jessica Berg, and Gwen Morton.

My brother, Tyler, who has music deep down in him like Grandma and Cyrus, is the guy I turn to for important playlists, and I'm thankful he was there to help me with the good foot-tapping music in this book too.

And to my very own 7, The Carleton 7. Jena, Katie, Lizzy, Mia, Wendy, and Zoe—you taught me how circles should feel: expanding and inclusive and constant. No matter to what towns or cities or countries our points spread, I always feel the tug of you.

And Kamahnie, Miles, and Paige—what an adventure we're having. If I know anything, I know that *you* are right where I belong.

Keep reading for a sneak peek at

Bea is for Blended

1

MOM MAKES ME PROMISE I won't bicker with Bryce today. So even though I caught him sneaking pepperoni off the platter before the ceremony, messing up the pattern of slices, I don't say anything. There's greasy evidence smudged on his rented tuxedo shirt, but I bite my tongue in the back of my mouth and remember how Mom looked right in my eyes and said, "Please, Bea. Not today," and how I looked right back in her eyes and said, "I got this."

My aunt Tam is reading a poem about new beginnings that makes me want to gag, and there are sixty-two people staring up at us with teary eyes. This isn't a new beginning, I think. It's a disastrous end.

At least I don't have to wear a dress or worry about

matching anybody else, because I'm the only one on this side. On my mom's side.

Opposite me, Cameron and Tucker and Bryce stand with their hands behind their backs. They match. Gray suits and blue bow ties. Bryce catches my eye and smirks and smacks his lips in a way that says I-know-you-know-about-the-pepperoni-but-you-can't-say-anything *so ha.* I squeeze both fists around the thick sunflower stems, and even though I want to blow the whistle, hold up a red card, and point him to the bench, today I just have to let the ball roll. Because today, my mom is marrying his dad.

I close my eyes when Wendell and my mom kiss, and open them when Wendell snorts. He always snorts when he happy-cries, and it'll be a while before he can stop. It's the same snort he has for sappy movie endings and those news stories when military parents come home and surprise their kids at school. It's the same snort that came from the way back of the gym during our end-of-year banquet, when Coach Wright talked about the importance of teamwork and how both coed rec teams had an incredible year of working together.

Wendell couldn't quit the snorting so he stepped out through the gym's double doors. I rolled my eyes at Nelle and Fern, the other two girls on my team, and Wendell missed when I got called up to receive the league's Most

Valuable Girl award. And when Bryce got Most Valuable Player.

Coach Wright handed us the awards and we had to stand next to each other so they could take a picture for the local paper. Nelle and Fern gave me little half smiles and I ran my fingers over the trophy. It was smaller than Bryce's. Everyone applauded but I knew what they were thinking. They were thinking I was more valuable than Bryce, and they were right, because I scored more goals, had more assists, and never got tired or needed a sub like he did. But, they were thinking, at least she got something.

Most Valuable Girl.

My eyes burned when I held the award and I wished Mom hadn't been called for an emergency at work because she would have stood up and said that this is *some bullsharky*. But I'll tell you one thing. I didn't cry. I bit my tongue in the back of my mouth and didn't smile for the camera.

I threw the trophy in the big black garbage bin on the way out.

The officiant announces that my mom and Wendell are married and Mom sends me a little smile because during the rehearsal last night she told him very clearly he was not to say *man and wife*. "We are man and woman, or husband and wife, but we are not *man and wife*," she said. The officiant nodded and made a note in his folder, and Mom crossed her arms over her chest and leaned into me for a secret Embers-girls fist bump.

At least she's not changing her name to Valentine. That is the last name on Earth to suit her, all heart-shaped and construction-paper pink. Even Wendell agrees that she's an Embers for life, bright and sparky and ready to ignite. And that's me too.

The organ player starts an upbeat song that fills the chapel and everyone stands and claps. Wendell pulls Cameron and Tucker and Bryce into a big Valentine hug and I can hear him whisper, "I love you boys so much." Then he puts his hand on my shoulder and smiles and hugs me too. He and Mom walk hand in hand down the three steps toward the aisle. Mom leans over to hug Grandma Bea in the front row and Wendell starts snorting again and wipes tears from his face. That makes Mom and Grandma Bea share a little Embers-girls laugh, not a laugh-at-him kind of laugh, but an oh-Wendell-you're-sappy-but-we-love-you-anyway   kind of laugh.

Mom leans into him and they start walking again. She's wearing a small sunflower in her dark braid and her dress is ivory and flowy and falls easily over the curve of her belly.

That curve is the reason for all this. They were going

to wait at least until Cameron and Tucker went to college. There was no rush, they kept telling us. They were going to keep taking it slow.

But now there will be another kid.

And I wonder which side that kid would be standing on if it were here. I wonder if it'll be a Valentine or an Embers.

Wendell kisses the top of Mom's head and puts his hand gently on her back. His finger has a new ring on it. It's different than the ring he was wearing the day he met my mom, the ring he just stopped wearing five years ago, the ring he keeps, with another ring, in a tiny blue porcelain container on his kitchen windowsill.

I watch his hand rub a small circle on my mom's back and my eyes burn, but then the officiant gestures for Cameron and Tucker. They throw their arms around each other's shoulders and move together down the aisle behind Mom and Wendell, waving to family in the first row. Everyone smiles at them in their matching suits and bow ties. Then the officiant signals to Bryce and me.

We step forward and meet in the middle, him in his gray suit and blue bow tie, me in my black swishy pants and red top, red like the US Women's National Team away jersey, red like embers. But I stay tight to my side of the aisle and hold the sunflowers between us. We are not on the same team, and he is not about to put his

5

greasy pepperoni hand over my shoulder, even if the officiant told us it would be nice for the camera. No way.

Mom and Wendell have their first dance and everyone
circles around with champagne glasses in their hands.
I'm standing between Grandma Bea and Aunt Tam and
the photographer squats in front of us and changes the
lens on her camera. Then flash! Flash! Flash! Flash! A
hundred little clicks make Mom and Wendell glow and
they're laughing at something that exists only in the little space between them. And I wonder if it's their new
baby. The only one of us who is both of theirs.

Then the music changes from slow and sappy to fast
and dancy and Wendell is opening his arms and waving
us all to join in. Aunt Tam is first. She hollers *whoo-
hoo!* and pumps her arms to the beat, and then Tucker
bounds into the circle and starts playing an air piano,
his fingers moving up and down the pretend keys, and
before I can think of how to get out of this I'm being
nudged out to dance too.

Grandma Bea holds both my hands and knows all
the words. *Ain't no mountain high enough!* She swings
my arms and it makes me move my feet and my pants
swish around my ankles. I don't really know how to
dance, but I'm good at soccer moves, so I pretend there's
a ball on the floor and do a couple of step-over-scissor
fakes. Grandma smiles big and sings, *To keep me from*

gettin' to you, babe! She's belting the song right to me and I don't mind that so much because it's better than looking at everyone twirling and mixing all over the dance floor.

This is exactly what Mom wanted. All this mixing. "No sides of the chapel," she told the wedding planner. "No seating chart. Just let everyone blend." She smiled up at Wendell when she said that last part. Bryce rolled his eyes and I did too and I think it was the first time we agreed on something.

As Grandma spins me around and sings at the top of her lungs about high mountains and wide rivers I'm thinking that's what people call us now. Blended. Except my side didn't get to add as much to the mix. It's been my mom and me from the very beginning. Now it's my mom and me and Wendell and Cameron and Tucker and Bryce. Plus, they have two dogs and one cat, Dodger and Roscoe and Fred. It doesn't seem fair, us adding two and them adding seven. Like the ref should blow his whistle and call a foul. *Too many players on the field!*

And I'll tell you one thing. If I got to choose one to send to the sideline, it'd be Bryce. I like him even less than the cat.

2

I DON'T UNDERSTAND WHY it's called a honeymoon. Mom never lets anyone call her honey, and they're not going to the moon. They're just driving to the Champlain Islands for two nights. But I wish they actually would go all the way to the moon, and stay awhile, because as soon as they get back Mom and I have to tape up our last boxes and leave the condo so we can move into a new house with enough space to blend.

I don't like sharing. Not one bit. And even though I don't have to share a bedroom in the new house, I have to share all the other rooms. It's bad enough already because Bryce has my same birthday and every year they make an announcement over the loudspeaker at school. *And a very happy birthday to Bea Embers and*

Bryce Valentine. And in fourth grade, when kids found out my mom was dating his dad, they started calling us The Twins. But I'll tell you one thing. I'm exactly six hours older than Bryce Valentine and I am not sharing any blended birthday parties with him. Ever.

When I wake up, I can hear Grandma Bea in our kitchen and I hope she's making pancakes. Hers are the best. Plus, whenever Mom is gone and Grandma sleeps over she adds M&M's to my breakfast because she knows they're my favorite and she gives me a wink like this is something we don't have to tell Mom. And I nod and smile, because even though I'm not one for secrets, this is one I'll keep.

I open my bedroom door and peek down the hall. Grandma's whisking batter at the counter. "Morning, Bea," she calls.

"Morning," I say and slide onto my stool. We only have two stools in the kitchen because we only need two, and I like it that way.

"I still just wish Mom would—"

"Bea," Grandma cuts me off fast and turns around with a dripping whisk. "Three."

I know I'm not getting around Grandma Bea's threes this morning. No one ever does. My mom did them every morning growing up, reciting three things she was grateful for before Grandma let her get out of bed, and that's how Mom has always woken me up too. *Good morning, Bea. What're your three?*

"Big or small," Grandma says. She pulls a pack of M&M's from the pocket of her apron, and gives me a little wink. "Three things."

I take a deep breath and think about the yard sale Mom and I found last week. "One, cleats that fit. Two, the soccer net for our new yard. And three . . . M&M's."

Grandma Bea spreads a ladle of batter on the griddle then looks me right in the eyes and says, "Those are good ones."

And that's the thing about Grandma Bea's threes. It's kind of like a time-out huddle. You might be down 2–0 with one minute left on the clock but a good captain reminds you of what you *do* have—like the best speed on the field, a strong left foot, or a secret weapon flip throw-in when you get within striking distance of the goal. And Grandma's a good captain.

She pours out five more pancakes and waves me over to drop in the M&M's. I make my soccer number, ten, on each one and Grandma grabs a spatula from the drawer. "Now, what were you saying about your mom?"

And that's the other thing about Grandma. She's good at reminding me that I have a lot to be grateful for, but she still listens to what's making me feel cruddy. Even lucky kids go through hard stuff, she says.

"I still don't understand why we can't stay in the condo. Mom and Wendell could just keep visiting each other." My M&M tens are getting all rainbow-melty. "The baby could stay with us, I guess. Or we could switch at halftime, when it turns nine or something."

Grandma chuckles a little and flips the pancakes. "I hear you," she says. "It'll be hard at first." She turns down the griddle and points her spatula at me. "But Wendell is good. And so are those boys." I want to tell her that she doesn't know Bryce and how he acts when he's around Kenny and Morris, but before I can, she says, "Your mom is happy."

I roll my eyes and Grandma rolls hers right along with me and says, "Oh, I know. It's total hogwash and Wendell's ruining everything."

I smile. "Exactly."

She pulls out two plates and slides three pancakes on each, then puts the jug of maple syrup on the counter, pours two glasses of milk, and sits down across from me on the other stool.

"Mmmmmmm," she hums after the first bite. "I love when your mom is out of town." That gets us both laughing and Grandma's laughs are like Wendell's snorts. They're hard to stop once they get started.

We blow bubbles in our cups and get enormous milk mustaches and eat with our fingers and talk with our mouths full and when we're done we leave the dishes in the sink and Grandma pulls me into her apron. "If you ever get sick of those boys and need some elbow room, you know what to do." I'm thinking she's going to say I can come visit her any time, but instead she juts her elbow hard like she's sinking it into Bryce's ribs and says, "Take it."

Then she gives me a look that says *you got this*.

Grandma's phone rings and she doesn't even say hello when she picks up, just, "You're not supposed to be worrying about anything, remember?" Then she pulls the phone away from her ear and mimics Mom blabbing. We snicker and I'm thinking Mom will ask to talk to me so I put my hand out for the phone and act like I'm annoyed even though I'm not because I kind of miss her too. But Grandma says, "OK, Louise. We will. Now go have fun."

She hangs up and says, "She wants us to go check on the boys. Make sure they're not running circles around their grandmother who is way, way older than I am." Grandma smiles and unties her apron and puts her hand on my shoulder. "Come on now, Bea, let's go make sure Grandma Ethel is still kicking."

I'm feeling like a starter who's been benched, and going to check on whether the Valentine boys are playing fair is the very last thing I want to do. But then Grandma says, "We'll stop on the way home for ice cream, because

we're going to need some dessert after that breakfast."
Like I said, Grandma Bea's a good captain.

On the way to the Valentines' house, Grandma says, "Let's take a detour down your new road," and turns right onto Evergreen. It's dirt, like most of the other roads in our town, but not like the condo that is walking distance from the village. The houses on Evergreen all have an upstairs, and garages for two cars, and front and back and side yards with trees separating them onto their own land. Even though we only live two roads over, it doesn't feel anything like this.

Our condo has one floor, and two bedrooms, and we share a carport and a wall with Aunt Tam. We share a yard with her too, and our back decks touch so she can just step over to our ours anytime and she knows how to let herself in. And even though I'm not one for sharing, I don't mind sharing with Aunt Tam. We moved into the condo when I was two weeks old so Mom and Tam have been friends my whole life.

Mom likes to remind me that as a baby I would cry and cry for what seemed like forever, like double overtime into penalty kicks, without quitting. "Always had that fire in you," she tells me. "You're an Embers all right."

On our first night in the condo, I cried and cried and nothing was working so Mom wrapped me in a blanket and walked outside in the cold Vermont air until my cries turned to whimpers and humming snores that sent little white puffs to warm the space between us.

And when I was sleeping like that, she tiptoed toward the back door and opened it to go inside, but I woke and cried, so she started over, walking the yard again, bouncing and shushing.

Then the light next door turned on and Tam shuffled out to the yard in her bathrobe and winter hat and big boots. Mom whispered she was so sorry and how embarrassing to meet our new neighbor this way, but Tam shushed my mom and put her arm around her shoulders and walked the yard with us. They took turns holding me, and running inside to make hot chocolate, circling the yard while I slept. And when the sun came up, Aunt Tam pushed my blanket down below my eyes and said, "Good morning, little Bea. I'm your Aunt Tam."

Grandma slows to a stop in front of our new house, number sixty-three. I look up the dirt driveway, and along the bricks of the front walk, and at the heavy wooden door, and it's weird to think I'll be sleeping in this house next week. And so will Wendell and Cameron and Tucker and Bryce and Dodger and Roscoe and Fred. And it's weird to think that Aunt Tam will be two streets away instead of just on the other side of my bedroom wall.

Grandma nods toward the house across the road. "You know your neighbors?" I shake my head. Their garage is

14

full of boxes and a mattress leans against a car in the driveway, but what I'm really looking at is one of those practice nets in the yard that's regulation goal-sized and sends the ball bouncing back to you. Before Grandma starts driving slowly again, the front door swings open and a girl I've never seen before comes bounding out with a soccer ball beneath her arm. She's wearing stretchy jean leggings and a button-down blousy shirt and her brown, wavy hair is long and loose over her shoulders, and she's barefoot. I'm thinking she can't possibly have any kind of good touch on the ball dressed like that.

Then she drops the ball on the lawn and starts striking it against the net and dead trapping its return every time before striking again. Hard. With her left foot.

I'm wondering if she's in sixth grade too and if she can do a flip throw-in and if she was the Most Valuable Girl wherever she came from.

"Looks like there's another soccer star moving to Evergreen Road," Grandma says. "Should we say hi? Feels like a good day to make a new friend."

"Nah," I say. "We better go save Grandma Ethel."

Mom always says it's important to find friends who'll walk with you through the cold night, even if you're walking in circles. But I'm not made of whispery, walky, hot chocolate hugs. I think I'm more like the icicles that hang from the eaves, strong and sharp and fine on my own.

I like Nelle and Fern from my rec team, but we're not the hang-outside-of-school kind of buddies. Plus, I do have one friend. And I don't need more than Maximilian.

The girl strikes the ball hard again and Grandma shrugs and we drive off, down Evergreen and onto Maple. The Valentine house is a five-minute drive from our condo and I don't know why Mom and Wendell think that's not close enough. When we get there, Cameron is taping boxes together in the driveway and Tucker is practicing his piano, which has been moved out to the garage already.

They wave and smile and walk toward us when we drive up. Grandma Bea pulls them into a hug. "We were just missing you and wanted to say hi."

Cameron kind of screws up his face like *really?* and so do I because we saw them yesterday, but Tucker smiles and gets all misty and I swear he's going to snort like Wendell. Then Grandma pulls me into the hug and I'm all squished in with them until she says, "OK, that feels better. Your brother inside?" They nod.

On the way to the house Grandma leans in for an Embers-girls whisper, "I do love those boys, but you can't tell a couple of teenagers you're coming to check on them." I smile and Ethel creaks the door open like she really is a hundred years old.

"Oh, hello!" she says. "Come in, come in."

I'm about to say we are just checking to make sure everyone is alive and we'll be on our way back to the condo now, but Grandma says OK and before I know it Ethel is inching through all the moving boxes and making tea and offering me a rice cake. I shake my head because rice cakes are dry and tasteless and only one-hundred-year-olds, and Wendell, like them.

I see the little blue porcelain container on their kitchen windowsill and I wonder where Wendell will keep that in our new house and I'm hoping not on our kitchen windowsill because that would feel a little weird and sad. I want to stop thinking about those rings inside so I start looking for Bryce and I know right where I'll find him because Wendell said, clearly, twice, "No video games. If you want to hang out with your friends, hang out with them in real life."

I open the door to the basement and hear the sound of explosions. I'm right. I don't even have to go down to check so I say, "Grandma Bea, Bryce is playing video games."

"And we had M&M's for breakfast," she says, and gives me that same wink like this is our little secret.

And I'm thinking, of course. Bryce gets away with everything. Little things like extra screen time and big things too.

Books by
LINDSEY STODDARD

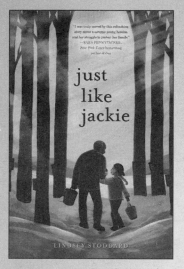